Books by Miriam Borgenicht

MARGIN FOR DOUBT

EXTREME REMEDIES

TO BORROW TROUBLE

DON'T LOOK BACK

RING AND WALK IN

CORPSE IN DIPLOMACY

Margin for Doubt

Margin for Doubt

Miriam Borgenicht

Published for the Crime Club by
Doubleday & Company, Inc.
Garden City, New York
1968

*All of the characters in this book
are fictitious, and any resemblance
to actual persons, living or dead,
is purely coincidental.*

Margin for Doubt

1

When the baby stopped crying, Jane went back to the kitchen to find that the noodles, predictably, had boiled over—she would have to pull the tray from under the stove and scour it. But not right now, though right now, before the stains had hardened, would be best. She had not yet washed the salad or browned the mushrooms, and she was counting on the mushrooms, when mixed with a leftover spoonful of fish, to keep Tony from noticing that a noodle casserole was all there was to supper.

However, Betsy discovered a new excuse for tears, so Jane was back at the crib, stroking, patting, when Tony came in. "Darling, something smells burning. Betsy, watch this." His accompanying gesture was also composite: a kiss that landed somewhat to the side of her mouth, a movement that pulled his pen from a pocket and waved it above the baby's puckered face.

"She's cranky. I could hardly keep her up till you got home."

"Silly faculty meeting—two hours to do ten minutes' work." His hand described waving circles with the pen, which Betsy's eyes were absorbedly following. "She feeling better?"

"Not really. Lots of sneezing since I took her to the doctor."

"Why didn't you have the doctor here?"

Because house visits are up to fifteen dollars and it's still only seven-fifty to go to his office. . . . Don't say it. Tony knows as well as you do. If that was the answer he wanted, he wouldn't have asked the question. "Such a nice day, couldn't possibly hurt her to be out."

"Look, baby. This way . . . No, here. Over here." As the

dance of the pen grew more animated, Betsy's expression became placid, content. Jane moved to the door.

"Come have a drink when she's quiet." A drink and the propitiatory mushrooms, to which she returned just in time. From the kitchen she heard the murmur of Tony's voice. It was the compelling kind of voice that could mesmerize classrooms, coax obdurate students into reading Keats, placate PTA presidents, and, more conveniently, seduce his own six-month-old baby into forgetting her stuffed-up nose. Furthermore, it was one of the features—like his good looks and his vast memory—about which he had no particular insight: she fell asleep, he would say in the tone of wonder he has used last night and would use again tomorrow night when he worked the accustomed feat.

"Guess what—she actually fell asleep." He was in the doorway.

Jane took off her apron and turned to him—this time the kiss was less abstracted. "School all right?"

"Fire drill as I was starting to give third period a test. . . . Um. Delicious. What is it?"

"Something to put you in a good humor."

"You cook lovely bribes." He leaned against the sink. "Everything okay here?"

"Fine." See: I didn't tell him how the druggist brought out our unpaid bills, I didn't even mention it, she said to whatever Providential accountant it was who supervised young marriage, kept score of wifely tact.

"Keep your hair that way—I decided I like it better."

It was her reward, starting already. "Have some more bribe on toast."

"Spoil my appetite."

"Nothing to spoil it for. Just these noodles." But from the look on his face, the incipient question, more explanation was needed. "The carriage fell apart on the way home from the doctor so I couldn't market."

"With Betsy in it?"

"Luckily I was on the sidewalk. Someone helped me hold it

till we got to the shoemaker, and he put one of those little pins in the wheel."

"Darling, it's ridiculous. You with a sick baby, carriage that comes apart."

"Come and eat."

"Go out tomorrow and get a new one. First-hand this time. What we should have bought right away."

"I—"

"Janey, love, I mean it. Suppose that happened in the middle of the street."

She hesitated. Was there some devious streak in her character which had started this conversation, or at least not tried to circumvent it? Had she wanted all along to get to this point, and should she, therefore, not take advantage of it? "If there's money for a new carriage I'd rather spend it on a rug because the place is awful without one." Steam rose from the colander, she felt it suffuse her cheeks.

"I'll take sandwiches for lunch next month, then you can have them both. Rug and carriage."

How quick he was to satisfy her, and how sweetly impractical were his solutions. She looked at him tenderly. "You keep right on having a decent lunch, you're skinny enough as is."

His hand reached out to put her free one on assorted portions of him. "This too skinny? This?"

"Tony! They can look in from across the way."

"They see it on TV."

She smiled, or would have if her mouth had been free. He was right: let them look. Indeed, when the two of them walked together across the lawn of the apartment house with the baby, or stood framed in a doorway, or appeared here between the kitchen curtains, she had the consciousness of them as a model couple, a prototype of attractiveness. Tony and Jane Bassett. High school English teacher, pretty wife. Dark head an appropriate three inches above blond. Brown eyes gazing down at blue.

But tonight she thought: model of money-pressed couple too. Tony had been home ten minutes, and they had discussed money—or gone out of their way to not discuss it—three times. On any night, it was their main subject. If they skipped the movies for a month, could they afford a new lamp? Should they have a dinner party, or should they save the money toward a week's vacation in June? When they had finished paying the doctor, could Jane buy the suit that would make her as well dressed as their neighbors?

That was the trouble, of course: their neighbors. Because Tony taught in Stoneycrest High School, they lived in Stoneycrest, which according to some statistics was the second richest but according to others only the third richest suburb in the country. Though Tony made a respectable salary of over eight thousand dollars a year, he made it in a place where everyone else, if you believed the awesome figures, had five times that much . . . ten times . . . twenty times. To a girl of clear vision and reasonable expectations, the discrepancies were startling: they squeezed their yearly budget into a sum that for most people around served to equip the yacht, or build a greenhouse, or furnish the den. When their baby was born with a defective heart valve that could be fixed but piled up expenses, the squeeze got tighter.

In a way, it was funny. She had always felt disdain for those who were preoccupied with money, she knew she could never be so preoccupied herself, it was exactly to discourage an emphasis on money that she turned down her first proposal. "Not exactly that I don't love you, Alan." She still remembered the judicious way she said it, and the earnest expression that showed the boy trying to work it out. "You have to admit, Janey—we do have fun together." "Oh, lots of fun." "Even better if we'd get married, you'd see." She nodded: vistas of pleasure opened before her. He reached for her hand. "You're so damn pretty, why can't you be sensible too?" However, being sensible was exactly what, at twenty-one, had seemed to her her strongest suit. She hesitated, sitting opposite him at the restaurant table. It was a table with a view; even as a college senior Alan knew how to manage head waiters. "Oh, Alan, all that money." "What money?" "That you're going to be making." His frown was a little less patient. "What kind of talk is that from an Economics major. A brokerage house—it's honest." "We'd be involved with money, don't you see? Stocks up, stocks down—we'd always be thinking about money." "Sorry I'm not a doctor, then we could think about cancer," he had said in anger but also implied concurrence. It was his fault too; he had given way too easily to injured pride; he should have told her that for all her great sensibleness, all those courses in Statistics and the Managerial Revolution, she knew nothing about everyday life. Because the fact was, of course, if you had plenty of money you could forget it, brush it aside. It was only if you were short of it that it colored everything, insinuated itself into every aspect of your day. You fell in love with a graduate student who was going to teach English, you saw yourself living in some rarefied intellectual atmosphere, and when he came home it was the difference between a second-hand carriage and a new one that dominated the evening.

She reached over to take his plate—then she saw how tired he looked. "Tony, I met Sheila in the elevator, she can babysit any night this week. Let's go to the movies."

He didn't answer; he was chewing on a roll.

"Darling, I'm dying to." It was what a wife had to do: not only get her husband to go out, but make it seem the going was for her sake, he was conferring a favor. "Please say yes."

He put down the bread. "Simon's leaving."

"Simon?"

"Yes, Simon," he said patiently. "My boss. He still isn't well from that operation, doctor says he has to quit."

"That means—"

"Um-hmm. Job is open for next year—head of the English Department."

She must not tremble or she would drop the tray. "I'm sorry about Simon," she said shakily.

He sat silent.

"Darling, how do you apply? I mean, what's the procedure?"

He picked up the roll again, buttered the piece that was

left. "You tell the principal and write a letter to the School Board. That's the whole thing—a letter stating your qualifications."

Her eyes rested on him. His qualifications. He was only the best teacher they'd ever had in Stoneycrest High. She knew it, of course, her love informed her daily, but he'd been there three years and everyone else knew it too. Parents intrigued to get him for their children. Students pleaded with their deans to let them switch to Mr. Bassett. Other teachers wondered audibly how he got those dumb bunnies to love Shakespeare.

"I didn't mean it about the movies, of course I don't mind staying home."

He was studying the empty bread tray.

"Now I think about it, Linda didn't like the picture at all, she said they—"

"We can drive to Staunton, see what's playing there."

"Darling, I didn't really want to go out anyhow. I mean, the letter. The letter to the School Board."

"Listen, Jane. I'm not writing any letter. I'm not applying for the job."

"But you—"

"Martin's the logical one to get it. He's been there seventeen years, he expects it."

"You mean you actually—"

"Job ought to go to Martin Cobden."

"But, Tony, he . . . you . . ." No. Stay calm. You can't do anything by sputtering, getting frantic. What he needs now is exactly your level-headed thinking. "Martin's bored with teaching. Sick of it. You've told me a dozen times."

"Seventeen years of pushing through those crowded halls. Listening to those moronic announcements on the loudspeaker. All that time he's taken for granted that he was next in line."

"Then he should have done his job better," she said coldly.

"He was a first-rate teacher once. He still could be. But after so long at the same routine—"

"Tony, don't you see, that's what can happen to you. I mean, suppose you hang around seventeen years."

"He wants the job for just a year, he said so today."

"After a year I suppose he'll go off lion shooting in Africa. Land some high-price job in advertising."

"I don't know what his plans are, I didn't ask."

She made herself draw a breath. There was a romantic streak in Tony, there always had been. It was part of what had attracted him to teaching in the first place, the element that, through whatever alchemy he generated in the classroom, was communicated to the students. But it was also the kind of streak that a wife had to moderate, balance with her protective good sense. Everything impractical and quixotic and generous in him felt the lure of making this sacrifice, and it was up to her to present the other side of the picture. "Suppose he decides to stay on."

"He said one year, he specified it."

"You have no proof."

"No proof, no guarantees. With Martin I don't need them."

She was silent; she realized suddenly there were alliances within a school for which no exact translation existed outside it. Tony and Martin were bound by everything that was maddening and wonderful about their work; they were part of a world of shared shop-talk, gripes, expectations, aims that no non-teacher could hope to penetrate.

"You've never been friends outside school. He and his wife live blocks away, and we never once had dinner with them, or went to the movies. They didn't send us a present when Betsy was born. And that silly wife of his—what's her name, Doreen?—that time at the tea, you hardly talked to her. You said she was a birdbrain, she made no sense."

His fingers were back at the bread again. Ink from the ditto machine always stained his hands—long after he washed, a little blue remained. Now the pellets of bread were turning blue.

"Okay, Martin's funny about his outside life. Evasive. Secretive. Maybe he does have some big secrets, I wouldn't know. He's your best friend till you get to the steps, but it ends there. You're walking across the parking lot with a stranger." His tone was quiet; a pellet of blue dough rolled across the table.

"But dammit, Jane, I like the guy. Can't you understand?"

She understood very well. It was easy to like Martin. He was, in fact, so likeable that the first time she met him at a faculty tea, having known only him and, of course, Tony, she got a distorted idea of high-school teachers, she thought they were all quietly humorous, cryptic, kind.

"Your husband's the luckiest break that's happened to Stoneycrest kids in a decade," Martin had said to her first thing, and she still remembered the comfortable feeling of being singled out by him, of knowing that someone experienced and intelligent was around to take stock.

"Tony says he couldn't last a week without you, you're wonderful to him."

Martin nodded. "They all need help at the beginning. But Tony has an instinct. When he's in front of a class, some magic gets across."

She stood there happily. She had been married two months, what could be more delectable than hearing praise about her new husband.

"He likes the kids too. He can actually treat an adolescent like a human being."

She stared across the room to where Tony was talking to one of the fifty-two faculty members whose names she would be expected to remember.

"Then there's the third attribute," Martin said. "The rare one."

"What's that?"

She was suddenly conscious of an equivocal quality about his look. "He's satisfied with himself. Our profession attracts the misfits—I guess you noticed. We're up there teaching about dangling modifiers, but what we're thinking is, when will we find a better wife, or a new personality, or another line of work."

"I didn't notice."

"Stick around, you'll see. Frustrated bunch, we teachers. We loused up our lives and we're stuck with them. We can't even— Listen, honey, forget it. I didn't mean it."

Some chill had gone over her—he must have noticed. But it all meant nothing. That ambiguous tone—he was the kind to mix cynicism with sincerity, offer the glib half-truths that drop with bright meaninglessness into the interstices of a party.

"Anyhow, your Tony doesn't know about frustration. He acts like a man who has exactly what he wants." He gave her his warm, not wholly avuncular smile. "Now, of course, I can see why."

He gave her his smile, but the ambiguities remained. Was it himself he was talking about? Was he someone who was stuck with a loused-up life? And was it an inevitable concomitant of this life that made him, as Tony said, evasive, secretive?

Now she looked at Tony across the table. "All right, Martin's bright. Interesting. But he's not you. He could never be the kind of teacher you are."

"Seventeen years . . ."

"Why don't you let the Board decide?"

"Can we have dessert, please? Can we?"

Even in her exasperation, she was careful not to make noise with the plates. They had not raised their voices either—Betsy slept on the other side of the room, past a divider which divided off everything but sound. They had thought of moving to a bigger apartment when she was born, but bigger apartments were forty dollars more a month, and rare besides. If you wanted a hundred-thousand-dollar house with a swimming pool, Stoneycrest agents could turn up a couple to show you—the advertising executives were always moving up or out or across the street—but if you had one of the few apartments, you did well to hang onto it. The divider had cost them fifty-eight dollars. Ten dollars for bricks, fifteen for lumber, seven for brackets, six for philodendron and ivy to fill in the open spaces, twenty for extra books which, since they were books they both wanted to read and would have bought eventually anyhow, were perhaps not strictly eligible to be itemized. She looked at it—a serviceable divider, and like their lives: a price tag on every segment.

"How much more does the job pay?" Her voice, she thought, was very steady. "Fifteen hundred? Two thousand?"

"Sixteen five."

"Martin doesn't even have a family. A childless couple— they don't have half our expenses."

"Must we keep on talking about it?"

"We could pay off the doctor. You could buy a decent raincoat."

"I don't mind skimping another year."

She picked up a pot and put it into the sink. It was not one of those pots with a strong bottom—you had to keep the flame exactly right or the food would burn. "It's me too. My life."

"Jane, please."

"Know how Betsy got this cold?—I didn't tell you. It was last Tuesday. That windy day—remember? I was buying a broom at Hardy's, and Linda came by, she said they're eighty cents cheaper at Lenox Discount. So I wheeled Betsy over there, and waited fifteen minutes on line, and then another twenty minutes to walk home, and by then it was raining. That slanty rain. Besides, it was only sixty cents—not eighty. So that was my achievement. While you were telling them about Petrarchan sonnets, I did my bit—I saved sixty cents."

She had never intended to say anything like this. She had meant only to convey the pinched quality that constrained their lives, the feeling of oppression that money problems imposed. But here was Tony staring at the wall as though detached from her, insensible. For a second she trembled: why had she gone so far? Then she saw the vein throbbing at the side of his neck, and a great sense of their marriage— of the stolidity of their marriage—came over her. As she moved beside him, he raised his head.

"I probably wouldn't get it anyhow," he said.

She suddenly felt faint; she held onto the table. "That Mr. Andrews—he'd put up a fight for you."

"He's only one—seven other School Board members."

"All you need—one man who'll tell what you did for his child." They both were talking quietly, as though conscious that a corner had been turned.

"Any other teacher—"

"Tony, she had any other teacher. All through school she had them, and when she came to you, she'd practically never read a book. And now which Ivy League college is she at? Which one?" But she stopped: she had done enough. "Here. Eat your fruit."

"Early for melon."

"Fruit man said I should try it."

"Doesn't he know you're married to a schoolteacher, you can't throw your money around?"

Any other time it would have been a standard jocular remark, but when she looked up, his face was drawn. Did it mean she had won, he would apply for the job? Fright fluttered suddenly along her nerves. Maybe she should never have meddled. So many imponderables when you touched other people's lives, so many surprises lying in wait. "Listen, darling—"

He was staring at the inadequate fruit.

"When I said all that . . . I mean, about taking the job—"

"That Betsy?" He was alert, anxious. "She crying again?"

"I'll go in to her in a second."

"You finish up here. I'll quiet her."

Win or lose? Which had she done? Which did she want? When she went in, he was still bending over the crib, patting those soft round shoulders, murmuring. "She'll sleep now, I think."

"You're a genius." She stood beside him, and again in this room—this half-room—with its smell of baby and talcum powder and damp blankets, she had the tremulous consciousness of them as a family, sturdy, insulated, absorbing. Did she want any changes? Was it right to think of changes? She moved closer to Tony in the conciliatory dark.

2

Was he doing the right thing, Tony thought. And whatever "right" meant, was it what he really wanted? He crossed the street, decided to call the whole project off, stepped on the curb, figured he might as well keep going. There was no scale for weighing the imponderables. Now that he knew he had the job, or at least he knew within four days he would have the job, was he sensible to consider giving it up? Three children passed, their faces relaxed into aimless giggling, and he looked after them longingly. When you were young, the decisions came easy. If a black card turns up. If the stoop has an uneven number of steps. But when a move concerned the destinies of at least four people, and might have implications that would transmit themselves for years, then no fortuitous signs were available—not even those most involved would offer any hint.

Certainly the front that Martin presented had been wholly impenetrable. "So you'll be head of the English Department. Congratulations." It was all he had said, when Tony stopped by his room after seventh period.

"It's not definite." He sat on a desk in the front row; it was one of the few desks the Stoneycrest School Board had not yet replaced with some artistically tinted and scientifically toughened formica—initials were carved in the wood.

"Definite enough. I guess Blair told you what he told me."

"He doesn't know for sure."

Martin brushed this aside. If the principal had talked to four members of a seven-man school board and had been informed by them of their impending decision, that was as much certainty as a school system ever proffered. Blair had called Tony in before school and presumably had also found time for a strategic five minutes with Martin. Blair didn't believe in pulling rank by withholding facts. He might, according to certain members of his faculty, grovel too readily before the parents and concentrate too emphatically on public relations, but if he had a way of curtailing suspense for one of his teachers, he would give the pertinent information to them, and just to them.

Martin leaned forward. "You'll run a good department. Great improvement."

"Listen, Martin. I really feel like—"

"Kids are wild about you. You get good work out of them. The best."

Was there bitterness under that flat conversational tone? But when he looked up, still no particular expression on Martin's face. It was a pleasant face; though flabbier than it should have been, flabbier than a year ago, Tony thought, it still wore the force of assertive intelligence on the high forehead, the sharp blue eyes.

"How many last year got into the college of their choice? After boning up with you in English 11?"

There was no truthful demurral for this, but no graceful assent to it either—baffled, he walked around the room. The wall decorations were like Martin—tired, run down, depressed. A student teacher had come in three years ago with big ideas about visual aids, and the pictures were the way she had left them: scotch tape joining the two halves of an English lane, paper curling over the inevitable flock of homeward-bound sheep, thumb tacks edging the sky where some pastel sunset had torn off.

"That idea you had about changing source themes. Ought to be a help."

He brushed chalk off his palms. Why was it always so hard for men to be sincere with each other? "Martin, I never would have applied if not for—"

"Do me a favor, will you?"

"What's that?"

"Next year get that damn book room in order. What a mess in there, I swear. *Vanity Fair* mixed in with tenth-grade anthologies. No poetry after nineteen-ten. And *Julius Caesar* —four different editions, you can't have a single class with the same page numbers."

"Martin, so many pressures—I don't have to tell you. Just that business with the baby, another year till we pay the bills."

"You were right to apply."

"I didn't even think I had a chance to get it." But this kind of fatuous disclaimer, he understood, constituted no exoneration at all.

"School Board has its ear to the ground, they know what to count on."

"That first year here, I couldn't work the ditto machine. I didn't know beans about discipline. Simon was no help, if not for you—"

"I saw Simon yesterday, he looks better."

Suddenly he realized that he was evading as much as Martin. "Listen, Martin. That business about your wanting the job for just a year. I don't get it."

"Skip it, Tony." Martin was running a pencil down his register, counting absences.

"I don't want to wait around like you did. Seventeen years —that's the honest truth. But if I could figure out why you—"

"Take the job. You'll have nothing to reproach yourself for."

Reproach. It was the least likely word for Martin to use, it had no connection with the set of ironic, mildly self-deprecatory terms with which he usually fended off inquiries.

"I don't mean a promise, nothing like that. But a year's delay—it does sound peculiar."

"I'm too lazy to be department head anyhow, everything would go to pot." Martin was the one walking now, he rubbed his hand over one of the posters.

"That's crazy." He spoke the more effusively in that it was also at least half true.

"Besides, I'm bored with Stoneycrest High. Fat lot of good I'd be for teacher morale."

"What are you—"

"Those books on the radiator—see them? Been sitting there six months. Every morning I think, today we'll get them out of here. Know when those books will move? Do you?"

"God's sake, Martin, I'm not trying to pry. That year business —you don't have to spell things out in detail."

"My judgment's impaired," he went on dreamily. "If there's one thing a department head ought to have, it's a sense of judgment in good working order. So now you see."

I don't see a damn thing. Did you tell me all this rubbish so I'd feel sorry for you, I wouldn't take the job? Or so I'd feel secure in my own superiority, I'd step right into it? Either premise had plausibility, either came complete with built-in rationale. "Martin, let's get this straight. I have no intention of—"

"Oh, Mr. Cobden." A girl came in, hugging her books against the bulk of sweater. "Mr. Cobden, I feel just awful, I know you said an extension till yesterday, yesterday was the last possible day, and really, I was going to have the paper in, I definitely was." The catalogue was a vehement one: a sore throat, a sick mother, definitely by the weekend, if only, but honestly, she appreciated so much. Breathless, impassioned, the promises poured out, and when she was finally gone, three minutes were left till the next period.

"How's Doreen?" He tossed a piece of chalk from one hand to the other.

"You know Doreen."

I don't know her. Not you, not your wife either. We live a few blocks away and I've hardly seen her. You've made sure of that.

Martin may have noted his expression. "Women. Little this, little that," he unhelpfully added. At the same time, he slouched back in his swivel chair with the familiar, negligent expression: sincerity over, it signaled—danger past. Tony edged toward the door. As Jane said, practically no chances for advancement in the system, you had to grab at what you could get. However, if the grabbing was going to leave you with this uncertainty. On the one hand. On the other hand. "Martin was no help at all"—it was what he had told Jane this afternoon. "If only he'd been angry. Blown his top. But nothing like that."

Her hands moved deftly. She had murmured something about the washing machine in the basement being broken again, broken till four in the afternoon, and great billows of diapers, shirts, sheets, pajamas lay around her on the bed.

"I said, he didn't get angry. Can't you hear?"

"You'll wake Betsy."

"Jane, I'm telling you Martin's reaction. All this indefinite stuff. I should get the book room in order. Buy standard editions of *Julius Caesar*."

"That sounds definite enough."

He looked at her figure, bent subdued, patient, over the interminable laundry, and irritation suddenly struck him. "Aren't you even interested? It was just for your sake I went after the job in the first place."

She stood so abruptly a pile of diapers fell on the floor. "That was a dumb thing to do."

"I didn't mean—"

"If that's the case, give it up right away."

"Oh, darling, it was silly, of course." He put his arms around her. "You know that, don't you?"

"Please don't do me any favors."

"Jane, forget it. It was for both of us, naturally. Jane, my sweet love . . ."

She was turning her head at last, letting him kiss her cheek, her mouth. His hands moved downward from her shoulders. With the money from the new job, they could move into a larger apartment, raise their voices at night, make love without the constraint of knowing every involuntary sound carried across a partition.

Easier on Jane too, he thought with tenderness. A less practical girl could toss off budget problems, let her husband worry about them, but Jane's competent mind, trained in college economics, was always reminding her that if they bought a vacuum cleaner they would not be able to cover payments on the car, or that a new dress for Betsy this week meant no movies for them the next.

"We can take a decent vacation. I'll still have to teach summer school, but those two weeks between. A place where you make reservations, and a crib is waiting for the baby."

"Be fine." She was examining straps on a shirt to see if it would take another washing.

"Staying around here—you don't feel you've had a vacation at all."

"I guess not."

He looked at her. Her hair hung forward, emphasizing the tired lines of her cheeks. And that striped blouse must be four years old—she had it the spring she met him in college. As they walked across the campus, sun would shine on her small compact figure, and the dozens of people who always seemed to know her would call a greeting, and he would feel an unaccustomed pride at the little skipping step she took to match her stride to his.

"The second things are settled I want you to go out and buy a new suit," he said heartily.

"All right."

"Something really good looking—you always say you want one. What color is it again?"

She pushed the blanket to one side. "You really don't like doing this, do you, Tony?"

"That Martin—he drives you crazy. You never know where you are."

She started on another pile of underwear.

"Is he really sore? Does he want it? And that business about pulling out after a year."

"I thought you were going to ask him today."

"You can't have a serious talk in school. Some substitute comes in, she can't find Angie's register, or a messenger from the office says where are your IBM cards, or a kid dashes in, all hysterical."

"How about after school?"

"I waited at three. But I must have waited at the wrong door, or the wrong time. Half the time he's not even around, he goes running off to New York."

"How come?"

"Education courses. Tuesday and Thursday—the kind of inanity you have to go in for if you want to move up in the system." The statement, sodden with accusation, hung in the room.

"Why would someone want a job for just a year?"

"Suppose it were something drastic."

"Drastic like what?"

"I don't know. His wife has a rare disease, she needs special treatment."

"Is she sick?"

"Little this, little that." He knew she was looking at him, without turning he felt the force of her gaze. "Okay, something else. He's been gambling, he's in a hole, he has to lay his hands on extra money."

"Extra money like sixteen hundred dollars?"

She still was not being any help. Usually, after a day of tense schedules and high-strung students, he loved her in that pose: head bent, expression patient, hands moving with automatic skill. But now he had again the spasm of annoyance —couldn't she offer the positive suggestion she knew he wanted? Must she leave it all to him?

"I'm going to try talking to him once more. I know he has strong feelings about privacy, but I'm involved too. His plans involve me. Can't I say that?"

"Sounds reasonable."

He watched her brush the soft strands of hair off her cheek. "And if he does make it clear that he'll quit after a year—"

"Then what?"

"Then I'll bow out," he said impatiently—where else did she think the conversation could lead?

"But you've already sent the letter of application."

"Meeting's not till Thursday—I can change my mind. Say I got an offer to finish my doctorate . . . write my thesis. What do you think?"

"Suit yourself, Tony."

"You're in this as much as I am."

She was bending away from the light, he couldn't even see her face. "If that's what you want to do, you might as well do it."

What you want to do. But did he know? Had he any certainty? When he paused to wait for traffic, he wiped perspiration from his face. It could be from uneasiness about the impending talk, but it could also be simply from the heat— it was one of the unnatural days in May that gave you a false expectation of summer, fooled you into thinking about beaches and vacation. He had been fooled himself today, held by the specious lure of both: weather that belonged to August, a job that belonged to someone else.

He turned down Mayhew. Though this downtown section held most of Stoneycrest's apartments, its shops were devoted to the inland estates and waterfront properties that surrounded it. HAVERMEYERS SKI SHOP. BOUTIQUE FOR FINE FURS. ARTISTIC FRAMING—BRING YOUR PRIZED ORIGINALS. GARNET'S DELICATESSEN, with cans of truffles and imported *paté* laid between green plastic leaves. A chauffeur in maroon uniform peered briefly at this display and went inside. For which of his students' families? For which seventeen-year-old who would not have prepared "To a Skylark" was a quick bite of *paté* on the way? He crossed another street, studied the signs. DORSET ARMS: GARDEN DEVELOPMENT. The garden was a few straggly junipers and some triangles of worn grass, but the entrance hall had ornate mirrors and a bank of artificial plants bedded in multi-colored stones. He was pressing a bell—COBDEN, 4F— when a woman came up.

"I have my key. You don't have to wait."

It was just as well—he had no desire to announce himself. Unexpectedness would be part of the impact: Martin must realize this was not one of those empty gestures made three minutes before the end of seventh period.

"Oh, yes, I agree." The woman, he realized, had been waiting. "—very hot weather for this time of year."

"Humid too. Terrible." She would stand on her rights; having opened the door for him, she could count on small talk in the elevator. "Probably going to rain."

"Weather report said clearing."

"You can't trust what they say." Her voice followed him through the closing door.

He walked down the hall. Nothing to reproach yourself for. Nothing to reproach. . . . After this visit, he would have nothing anyhow; he would try once more and then let it rest. He drew a breath, in air heavy with the smells of supper. Which apartment? Not this one, surely, with roller skates, a bicycle, rubbers in front of the door, and a chorus of noise coming through it. No noise from 4F. No noise, indeed, even after he rang. Could they be out, at seven-thirty on a Monday night? The movies? A friend's house? A restaurant? He and Jane were so bound to the routine of the baby, it had not occurred to him everyone else was not similarly encumbered. A childless couple—nothing to keep them home. He rang again: he could go through it now, but this resolve was just tenuous enough so it might not bring him back tomorrow, even later tonight.

"Martin?" Above his voice, more noise from the door across the hall. A child peered out, said mysteriously, "Still two and a half hours," and brought in a pair of rubbers. In the new silence, he rang again. Maybe this was the sign he had been looking for earlier: Martin was out, he could keep the job.

However, there was always the chance the bell didn't work—a bell had not worked for them all last March till the electrician was finally summoned by a reluctant landlord. He reached for the knob, turned it, walked in.

"Martin? Anyone home?" He blinked, standing in the doorway; you saw a man every day in his classroom, who would guess he came home each night to a place with flowered curtains, little cut-velvet pillows, paisley chintz? All that busy work, Jane would say—as if seeing it through her sensibly critical gaze, he passed judgment. And what kind of kitchen, to go with all this? He would take a quick look, so his report to Jane would be complete: more cute little nonsense, he would tell her. He was right about the cuteness: copper cookie-cutters on the wall, frilled pink-and-green edging along the shelves, matching canisters in a row on the table. And next to them, sitting at the table and yet not quite sitting, with his head slumped down and his hands hanging grotesque and lifeless alongside the table's chromium legs, was Martin.

3

"My name? How do I spell it?" It had its ludicrous aspects: a man might be dead in the kitchen, and this police sergeant at the other end of the phone was inquiring whether Bassett had two S's or one.

"That's right. Double S, double T." Then, for the first time, Tony realized how involved he was himself. Before this he had considered only the need for haste: they must come fast, he was sure but not entirely sure, maybe if they got here right away. But now his own position struck him. He had come over here to get free of obligation, or at least to win inviolability for his conscience, and by having found Martin, he was now bound up with him, snared in his troubles, trapped.

"Tony for Anthony?"

"No, just plain— Listen. You sure someone's coming quickly?"

"On the way, on the way. Now, about that empty glass again."

"Yes. It was right there next to him on the table. With some drink with a deep red color—Campari, maybe. He'd drunk almost the whole thing." He heard himself with wonder. He had not realized he was noticing anything, he had thought only the unseemly form slouched across the formica table had entered his consciousness. But when he called the police and started talking, his mind, he found, held a precise picture of the scene: pork chops laid out in brown paper on the sink, scalloped gold decorations on the glass which held what was left of the drink, melted remains in the ice bucket. And, of course, the color on Martin's face, which, together with the clammy skin, the smell, gave to even an uninformed spectator the unmistakable message of poison.

"They'll have stuff for taking care of him?" he asked clearly. "If it's not too late?"

"All the equipment. Yes." A pause from that crisp voice at the other end, then indistinct noises. Was the man taking notes? Giving emergency orders to a car already started? Or had he just reached for the sandwich in his lower desk drawer —was this as good a chance as any to finish an interrupted lunch?

"Is there anything—I should do?"

"Sure you don't know where Mrs. Cobden is?"

"I have no idea, I told you. . . . Yes, I'll wait."

He waited with his hand still on the phone, his gaze disbelieving as he stared at a picture of nymphs and cupids, at lavender pillows lying plumply on lavender and turquoise chairs, at turquoise rugs with fringed border side by side on the floor. Wait—of course. But wait here? Wait in the chill incongruity of a turquoise-and-lavender bedroom? He went to the front door, keeping his eyes averted so he would not have to corroborate that view in the kitchen. The noise from across the hall was louder; not so much screaming, he felt like telling those insensitive children. He had to talk to someone—when the elevator came and two people got out, he could hardly keep from calling to them. Suddenly the import of Doreen's absence struck him: he would be the one to tell her. She would come back from shopping for a last-minute dessert, she would get off the elevator and walk quickly because it was late, those chops ought to be started. Don't take those packages into the kitchen . . . was there some other way to say it? He held his breath while the clanking of pulleys announced that the elevator was again on the way up, was approaching the floor, was past it.

"Still two and a half hours. Maybe three." The child was wearing a terry-cloth bathrobe as she opened the door this time, stooped for a pair of skates.

"Two and a half hours till when?" But she had retreated

again into that unrelenting roar. My turn. Ellen's turn. No, my turn. Just you wait till Daddy . . .

He moved closer. Three children, from the sound of it. Three children who must on all account be kept inside, shielded from whatever equipment, paraphernalia, horrors, would shortly be gone by . . . that door had to stay closed. However, it was opening again. Another child—younger but with the same high forehead above a round-eyed stare—reached toward the tricycle. "Promise not to bust the lamps if I get it?" she called.

"What's two and a half hours?" he said.

"They're sometimes wrong, it could go much faster now."

"That's fine." His smile, however, elicited only the familiar withdrawal—like her sister, she performed it with a motion that seemed about to decapitate her, pulled her head in at the last possible second.

"Tell Doreen," a voice shouted over other noises.

"Where's Doreen?"

"Doreen's sitting." He was again regarding a closed door—after a second, he walked over and opened it.

"Watch out. It'll run you over." The warning was issued about the newly delivered tricycle—its rider circled the rug, made a dent in a table leg, missed his own leg by inches, ran over an edge of curtain, and started another circuit. He looked around the room. Wrong about only three children, he thought. Counting the two who had come to the hall, and the mad bike rider, and two others on the couch, there must be five—no wonder there was so much noise.

"Is Mrs. Cobden here?"

"Who?"

"He wants Doreen."

"She's helping Lorie bathe the baby. In there."

In there, he found presently, was a room to the left—Doreen sat watching while the girl in the terry-cloth bathrobe was lathering soap over a naked child.

"Doreen, listen. Could you come out to the hall a minute?"

Her face had been puzzled as it followed the actions with soap and washcloth—now it stiffened into total bewilderment.

"Remember me? Tony Bassett. I teach with—I'm at Stoneycrest High."

"Stoneycrest . . ."

"So then you wrap the towel like this and she can't fall off or get cold, see." Despite his preoccupations, his paternally trained eye noted that Lorie's palm was secure against the baby's stomach, the washcloth lay safe in a basin, the towel covered the pink nakedness. The baby must be older than Betsy—ten months, maybe a year.

"Yes. I see." Submissive, absorbed in the bath lesson, Doreen spoke respectfully. Then she looked at him. "Anything wrong out there?"

Another crash from the bicycle course. Did the curtain go down? A lamp? "No. Nothing wrong." His mouth was dry. "Could you come out in the hall for a minute. It's important."

"She can't leave." Lorie reached for talcum. "She's bathing the baby."

"Looks to me as if—please. Just for a minute." It was to Lorie, he realized, that he had put the request.

"She's sitting for us. She has to stay." While Lorie issued the decree, Doreen picked up the washcloth, twisted it, saw that drops were falling on the rug, put it back. She had on a pink eyelet dress and charm bracelets.

From the next room he heard a phone ring; then a new face appeared in the doorway. "Five minutes apart. Only with Henry she lasted that way two hours."

"It was Lance."

"Was not, I remember distinctly. Henry."

It was no use: he went back through the living room, evaded the cyclist, crossed the hall. Authority, finally, had arrived: two figures—a policeman? a doctor?—were bending over what lay on the floor.

He stood back from the doorway. "Is there any? . . . Can you still? . . ."

"Fifteen **minutes** after he took the stuff you couldn't help him." It was the doctor who came out, followed him into the living room, stood a minute with his surprised gaze held by a shelf of china cats. "You Mr. Bassett?"

He nodded. "What was it?"

"Cyanide, probably, from the signs—we'll know for sure after the autopsy. Also, there's an empty bottle of it in the kitchen waste basket. Considerate."

Of course—that was Martin all over. A damn considerate fellow. So considerate he'd tell you beforehand you had nothing to reproach yourself for.

He felt the doctor's look. "Cyanide," he repeated. A small bottle: that would do the trick. The size bottle a man might carry in a brief case, next to his test papers on *David Copperfield*, his IBM class lists. And what about buying it? Would he go in for aimless chatter about the weather, to deter the suspicions in advance? Would he offer to the uninquisitive druggist some gratuitous story about insects on the plants.

Plenty of plants, in any case, in fluted pottery pots on the window sill—revolted, he turned away. "Can you tell how long ago it happened?"

"An hour or so. Maybe less." The doctor peered again around the room, as if the answer to a man's suicide might be found in a ball-fringed lamp shade, a velvet pillow in green and orange.

It wasn't his taste, he wanted to say. Not a goddamn thing in this ridiculous room he'd have picked out for himself. . . . Wrong. Something else he wanted to say more. "Listen. What makes everyone so sure it was suicide?"

"They're not."

"Who said it was suicide anyhow?"

"You. You're the one. You mentioned it first."

"Well, then, maybe . . ." No. Quit trying to find loopholes. A man alone in an apartment—a considerate man—swallows enough cyanide to kill himself in fifteen minutes: what can you hope for except suicide? What miracle of contrivance or well-planned accident do you think will be discovered to get

Tony Bassett off the hook? Suicide—remember that. Martin's suicide, to reproach you all your life.

"You a relative of his?" Businesslike, even bored, the doctor was winding it up.

"Just a friend. Colleague."

"He expect you?"

"I just happened—I was coming in to see him."

"No one else around?"

"His wife is right over there. Across the hall. I've been trying to tell her."

"You better do it fast. Unless you want her to hear from the police."

"I'll go back. I'll do it." But it was only because he felt on his back the impersonal force of that gaze that he could make himself again cross the hall, open the door, intrude into the anomalous gaiety of that apartment. Though the bike rider had quit, another child—still another one?—was putting on skates. He was suddenly aware of more activities, unexplored rooms: "Tell Doreen I'm taking the lamb out of the oven," someone called from the right—stolid, he turned left, toward the bath lesson.

"Doreen has to come with me right away. It's imperative." He spoke directly to Lorie—she was sprinkling powder under the baby's knees.

"She has to stay till the baby's born. Might be all night, Daddy says."

He had the absurd notion to give the news to Lorie, let her break it to Doreen. Lorie could handle things perfectly and still not interrupt the masterly motions with which she held the baby, powdered it. "Lorie, listen. Isn't there someone else in the house? Someone to take care of you." He sensed, without turning, that the usual line of spectators was gathering at his back.

"Mrs. Malley sometimes comes down, but Mom said never again."

"You." He turned quickly, pointed an arbitrary finger. "Get Mrs. Malley. Tell her it's an emergency. Life and death."

"Last time her twins made all that mess in the kitchen."

Two more children in here, he thought—how could it possibly matter? "Go on. Scoot. Don't waste a second."

"Anyhow, no one dies in childbirth, Daddy says so, we don't have anything to worry." Lorie's voice carried a distinct rebuke.

"Okay, chicken. You're right." His hand went out, for a second, to her shoulder—then he turned to Doreen. "Mrs. Malley will be here. Or someone. These children will be fine. I want you to come with me."

Like a child herself, however, Doreen pulled back. "Something's wrong. I can tell." She was retreating toward the bed, behind it—her hand pulled at a tuft in the candlewick bedspread. It came off in her fingers, a small yellow puff, and her perplexed look fastened on it.

"Everything's fine but you have to come."

"You're just pretending."

She must not give way to crying here. These children had great powers of acceptance: the fallen curtain, the overcooked meat, the wildly careening bicycle . . . all were within their tolerant limits, but tonight of all nights they must not see an adult's hysteria. "Nothing wrong, but I have to talk to you. Without anyone listening." It was his school-teacher voice, reassuring but not susceptible to argument.

Her hands, with the charm bracelets clinking, tugged at the loop of her dress. "I don't want anything to be wrong."

"Doreen, listen—"

"I can't bear it."

What she meant, he understood suddenly, was that she couldn't cope with it. Whatever it was going to be, she couldn't cope. Not with bathing this child, not with taking meat out of the oven, and not with her husband's untimely death. He, Tony, would have to cope—his involvement was only starting. It was only fair. Martin must have shielded her, cared for her, and the job must now fall on the shoulders of the man who bore a direct responsibility for Martin's death.

4

"Some toast, Doreen? Cheese? You have to eat something."

"I just couldn't. I'd be sick." Indeed, Doreen looked sick now, with her cheeks swollen from weeping, her eyes red, her curls tangled outside the butterfly barrette.

"Well, drink some coffee. It's fresh." It had to be; she had long since finished washing up, sweeping, drying, she was sewing straps on Betsy's outgrown underwear when Tony and Doreen came in.

"Jane's right. You need some food."

"Honestly, you two are both so good to me, I never met such good people in all my life."

It was, of course, an exaggeration; they were doing, Jane thought, what any people would do after a girl's husband had committed suicide. If they were utter strangers, they would do it. However—the thought persisted with an insidious chill —they were not utter strangers, or, rather, they could not continue being so. They were now so involved that Tony's face, far from wearing its usual look of appealing vigor, was gray, almost ashen. She looked at him with great compassion. He had had a terrible time: not simply to find a dead body— the body of someone you knew—but to have to escort the distraught wife to the police, help her make statements, sustain her. And under the circumstances, naturally, there had been no choice, he had to protect Doreen, but he was the one who needed protection now. She leaned forward.

"Do you have a family, Doreen?"

Doreen sucked at the cord of her dress. It was a pink eyelet dress with short sleeves and a wide scoop neck; the loop in front was damp from being in and out of her mouth. "My father died last year. My mother's in kind of, you might call it a rest home. This little town near Bennington, Vermont. Where I used to live."

"I see."

"I have this brother but we really don't keep track of each other. He travels. He's in the pocketbook business, he's always finding some little place in Hong Kong or Peru where they can stitch things together cheap. You'd think with all the sewing machines in America. Anyhow, last I heard he was— well, across some ocean."

"How about Martin's family?"

Vague, stunned, Doreen lifted her sodden face. "Oh, them!"

"Martin didn't get on with them?" Tony asked.

"That's it." Doreen spoke with alacrity.

"Get on or not, you have to call them tonight," she said, crisply practical. "Right away. This minute."

"They live in California. The time's all different there— maybe two or three o'clock in the morning right now, I'd be waking them up."

"No. The time's three hours earlier. They'd just be finishing dinner, probably." Though her heart ached for Doreen, she was conscious of a small critical impatience under the sympathy. Don't be so inept, she wanted to tell Doreen—Tony can't bear ineptitude, it drives him wild. He's good and generous, there's no man in the world with more sweet goodness than he has, but he gets furious when students are unnecessarily thoughtless or foolish, and he doesn't like to meet these traits in anyone else either.

Doreen was sobbing again. "I couldn't bear to talk to them tonight. I just couldn't."

"I know it's hard, Doreen, but we . . . we're . . ." How should she say it? Without seeming to disavow or even diminish the sympathy she and Tony gave, how express the unsuitability of their being the only ones to give it? For Doreen to be sitting around a table with people who hardly knew her, who had talked to her once at a faculty tea—it was improper, almost. A desecration of what should be a time of great solemnity. "Families . . . people who are close . . ." she started again, but Tony interrupted.

"Of course wait till tomorrow if you'll feel better," he told Doreen soothingly across the kitchen table.

She put the coffee pot down hard on the sink. "Well, who did you call?"

"All those terrible questions from the police, and the reporters. I was so mixed up. I mean, I suppose they have to know at school. The principal. Someone."

"I'll take care of that," Tony said quickly.

She went over to the door, but not a sound—for all this unaccustomed clatter, Betsy was still asleep. "Listen, Doreen. Don't you have friends who'll be hurt? Angry if they aren't called? A time like this—people want to help, really."

"We don't have any close friends. Martin was so busy, his courses and all. And school. School was his whole life, just about."

School was not his whole life. School wasn't even enough of his life to let him be a good teacher. In fact, the reason we're so involved in all this is that Martin was negligent about school, so Tony got the job. But if she, Jane, knew all this, wouldn't Doreen know it too? And if she was lying about this, on the night of her husband's death, what else would she lie about?

"So you have no one really close?"

"She has us," Tony said.

Jane rubbed steel wool across the stain on the drain board, and when she turned, Doreen was regarding her wistfully. "I think I'll have that sandwich now. If it isn't too much trouble."

"No trouble at all." She had, in fact, after Doreen's third refusal, thrown the sandwich away—she would have to make a new one.

"I didn't have dinner. We were just . . . I was . . . the pork chops . . ." Fresh tears threatened.

"If only I'd skipped dinner myself," Tony said. "If I'd gone earlier."

She couldn't bear to see that look of self-reproach on his face. *Tony darling, we're in this together, I made you go after that job. . . . if only she could say it. Or if she could touch him. If she could move her hand, put it lovingly over his upturned one as it lay on the straw place mat.* But of course, in the presence of Doreen's grief they must show no affection toward each other, even the smallest show of sentiment would be wrong. "Why didn't Martin tell me? Just a hint," Tony said miserably—"all I needed. Something to let me know the goddamn job meant so much to him."

In the silence that followed, Doreen began to cry again. The tears welled up, the pink loops got wetter, and she had an insistent thought. *Doreen doesn't know what Tony is talking about. If Tony doesn't specify the job, it might just turn out that Doreen has no idea what it is.* Her eyes went to Tony's troubled ones. *Don't say anything,* she signaled to him, shaking her head very slightly. It was all but imperceptible, but imperceptible signals were all that had ever been needed between them.

"All he had to do was say it. Tony, I want the job of department head—just that. For once let someone know his feelings under all that detached air."

When she had turned off the dripping faucet, she was conscious of the stillness, not just here in the kitchen, but outside. Though their windows opened on a main street, there was little weekday night activity in this suburb where most people were commuters: not a horn sounded three stories below in the street. "Doreen, listen. That business of a year—Martin's wanting the job for just a year—what was it about?"

"I don't know."

"He didn't tell you?"

"He didn't say anything." Doreen gave a little sniff.

Was it true? Could it possibly be true? While she heard Tony's voice explaining the facts with laborious patience—he had just been coming over to have things out with Martin, he didn't want a job someone else desperately needed—while this earnest recital went on, she was assailed again by the qualms. If Doreen didn't know, how come she didn't know? If a job was important enough so a man would commit suicide over the disappointment of not getting it, wouldn't his wife be informed about the circumstances? Did it mean the estimate of a year was a false one? Or were there other reasons for Martin's despondency—reasons that had nothing to do with a high-school position, and that would entirely alter Tony's obligation?

And if all this was so obvious to her, why couldn't Tony see it too? "Did he say anything about Tony's being in line for the job? Did he tell you that today?"

"I didn't see him today. I was just waiting, and then all of a sudden that excitement across the hall. The children yanking and pulling, I had to go."

"They're a strong-minded bunch," Tony confirmed.

"How many are there?"

"Eight"—then he looked at his watch. "No, nine, I guess, a few hours ago the pains were five minutes apart."

She could picture the incongruities of that scene: the hilarious children, the nervously rushing mother, the next-door neighbor pressed, without ceremony or option, into service. She knew the timetable too; the police, it appeared, had gone over it thoroughly: six o'clock, Doreen's recruitment by the frantic family, which thereafter kept her wholly, assiduously occupied; six-thirty, Martin's return home through the apartment-house lobby, where he spoke to a Mrs. Landesman with her dog, a Mr. and Mrs. Tracy who had just arrived suntanned from the beach, a Heller child who was looking for a missing sneaker; seven o'clock, or a few minutes either side of it, the drink of Campari plus a sufficient amount of potassium cyanide; seven forty-five, too late to do any good, Tony's arrival.

The timetable, yes. But not the reality. Not the inner truth to bring a story to life. I don't believe it, she thought suddenly. I know the facts bear it out, and Tony has swallowed it whole, but I still don't believe it. Something doesn't fit, and if Tony weren't wrapped up in guilt, if guilt had not suspended his judgment, he would see this too.

Oh, my darling, don't jump so fast to feeling guilty. . . . she turned on the water to wash the coffee pot; these doubts must be saved for when she was alone with Tony. How long till that would be? One hour? Two? It was essential for them to be alone. Vital. It wasn't that she would change Tony's ideas—things had never been like that between them—but when he told them to her he would automatically scrutinize them himself, qualify them, see them from another viewpoint. Something doesn't fit . . . he could come around to it. But that had to happen fast, before his convictions stiffened, went beyond his own control to alter them.

"When you went to sit with that family, did Martin know where you were? Did you leave a note?"

"There was no time. The way they grab you, those children. All that rushing."

"So he might have thought you'd be home any minute."

"Jane, she doesn't want to talk about it, it's all too painful."

That was not exactly true either, she thought. The fact was, Doreen looked better: she was drawing vitality from the conversation. Despite the tears that had been pouring out for an hour, she was brighter now than when she came. However, it was terribly late. Past midnight. She and Tony rarely stayed up this late. She herself had struggled through the first onslaught of weariness, she was now in that state of nervous second wind which would take its toll when she tried to go to sleep. She could nap tomorrow when Betsy allowed, but what about Tony? What about his nerves when the alarm rang, he had to get off to school?

Then she understood: the alarm would not ring, he would not go to school. All those plans—arranging the funeral, calling relatives, studying bank accounts—he was going to help Doreen with them. Tony never missed school. It was part of the mystique of teaching that you kept to its schedules, you allowed yourself no excuses, you adjusted to a day bound by

IBM programs and bells that rang every forty-six minutes. He had gotten to school on time when the fan belt broke on the car, when a doctor diagnosed Jane's sore throat as pneumonia, when the movers phoned that the van with their furniture was mistakenly sitting in Stoneycrest, Ohio. Quarterly test on *Macbeth*, he would say, as he went off with a red nose and a forehead burning with what she was sure was a one-hundred-and-three-degree temperature. Even Betsy had been tuned in: she had postponed her birth until ten o'clock on a Saturday morning. But he would miss school tomorrow. And what else? What other changes were in store?

She washed the sink and went in to cover Betsy, and when she came back Doreen was still talking. ". . . really fierce moods. Sometimes he wouldn't say a thing. I'd tell him some funny story—you know, the carts getting stuck in the supermarket—but even then." Her ingenuous expression consulted them. "But some men are like that, aren't they? Moody. Quiet."

"Of course, Doreen, they really are."

"So I shouldn't have done anything. Like take precautions? Be careful?"

"You couldn't possibly know, don't think about it."

"Besides, when someone's older, you don't feel you can tell them how to act."

Attentive, they waited.

"I mean, Martin was forty-two. And I won't be thirty till August." With her hair smoothed down, her face composed, Doreen looked even younger.

"Even a moody man of forty-two, if he was going to commit suicide, you'd think he'd leave a note." She had not intended to sound so tart.

"But there was a note, didn't you know?" Doreen said brightly. "The police figure he must have been working on it, and when he couldn't get it just right, he left it."

She turned to Tony, but he was nodding too, confirming Doreen's evidence. "What did it say?"

"'Have to do this' . . . that's the way it starts, not even

a capital letter. 'Have to do this, I've thought and thought, there really is no alternative. When you are alone'—no, 'When you're alone,' that's the way he put it, I remember—'When you're alone I think you should go back to Vermont. Stoney-crest is no place for you, don't try to live here. You will be much better off up there. Some day you may even be glad that I'm not around to—' "

To what? Why must Doreen stop now? Then she realized the stopping was not because of Doreen's revived tears but Martin's cavalier abruptness. "That's all he said?"

"Not even his name signed. But his handwriting, all right, they know that for sure."

"Where was the letter?"

"Right in with his papers. His top desk drawer where he kept his bills."

Did this inauspicious location for a suicide note have any significance? Did it, indeed, change her doubts—that cloudy, incomplete, unforthright statement which Doreen rattled off as if she had memorized it, she even had a kind of relish in it? "Where in Vermont?" she asked, conscious of the dull quality of her own voice against the sharpness of Doreen's.

"This little town. Harrod, way down in the southern tip. You probably never heard of it, but Martin came up for the mountains. He loved mountains. If there was a view, he had to get on top and see it."

"I didn't know he went in for climbing," Tony said.

"He hasn't since we're married, of course. But before that, no matter what the weather. That's how it started. He came to this hotel because it's right smack on the Appalachian Trail, and I was working at the desk. Assistant Manager, sort of."

Receptionist, Jane's mind provided. It also provided a picture of the background: sun setting behind pine trees, path twisting through the woods, sign promising 3.2 miles to summit . . . all the paraphernalia to delight a tired schoolteacher, bring him up after a week of bells and schedules. But what about the rest of it? Did this girl with the empty prettiness delight him too? Was there indeed a time when Doreen's chatter had appealed to Martin, seemed to him what he was looking for? And if he was so fond of climbing before marriage, why "of course" had he given it up afterwards?

"This place . . . Harrod . . . I guess you'll be going back there now," she said politely, but Doreen shook her head. The last thing she wanted to do was leave Stoneycrest. She just adored Stoneycrest. No matter what Martin said, Stoneycrest was where she wanted to stay. She would never find anyplace else so beautiful.

Her round eyes questioned them. "Don't you think it's beautiful?"

"For some people."

"All those gorgeous homes, if you drive along any street you see them. And the shops. I go window shopping every afternoon, just about."

She said nothing; she wiped a glass.

"And that waterfront, with all the yachts."

She couldn't help herself. "Suppose you don't have a yacht."

"Martin had a sailboat, he tried to teach me but I never caught on. All that to remember—ropes and jibs and pulleys. So he sold it and got this cute motorboat." Doreen lifted her innocent gaze. "Much better, don't you think?"

"I guess so."

"And our darling apartment, all those materials I got to match. Everything's perfect now—how could I possibly leave?"

The sobs were mounting again—at last Tony looked up. "Doreen must be tired."

"Yes." A brief silence, transfixed in indecision. She stared at Tony's eyes, under the bushy eyebrows. When his eyebrows looked like that, she would wet the tip of her finger on her tongue, rub it over those bristly hairs. Hold still, you look a disgrace, her loving voice would murmur. Now she leaned toward the door. "I wish we had room. But our extra bed is in there with Betsy, and it's so . . . it's . . ."

"But I love babies, I really do. I couldn't have one, after

the accident, but I always said, if there's anything cuter than
a baby."

What accident, she almost said—then she realized she didn't
care. She didn't need to know. The last thing she wanted was
to get that metallic voice started again. Whatever had happened between Martin and Doreen, she had heard enough,
all she wanted was to be alone with Tony. In a second they
would be alone. Tony would explain about the partition, the
device that looked so good, with its plants and books and
vases, but in the way of soundproofing accomplished nothing
at all. In fact, he had pushed his plate aside, he was standing
too.

"Of course Doreen can't go back to that place alone."

Well, of course Doreen couldn't. It was obvious. Tony could
not be righter: Doreen couldn't spend the night in that apartment. Just because she herself had taken for granted that after
the strained moments and tight silences they would be able
to fall at last into that intimacy which night after night restored them, settled things, erased the misguided words and
made new ones unnecessary . . . well, Tony was right. Of
course.

"I'll be in your way." Doreen was still crying.

"Not in the least, how could you possibly?" They would
have to lie stiffly, one on either side of the bed, conscious
that every sound could go past the philodenron leaves, the
set of *Dickens*.

"This dress—"

"Jane will lend you something. You get right in there,
Jane'll give you everything you need."

Absolutely right—how could she not have seen? There was
not even an alternative. "Come on, Doreen, I'll show you
the room."

5

"I don't know how I can ever thank you." Doreen's trusting gaze was turned on him.

"Please don't."

"All the wonderful things—"

"Nothing wonderful. Besides, I want to do them."

"If I didn't have you, what would become of me?"

"Doreen, you promised. No crying this morning. We'll take care of everything, but no crying."

They had taken care of plenty already. Funeral arrangements for next Saturday, so Martin's brother from California would have plenty of time to come. Another meeting with the police, who released the medical examiner's report that Martin had taken, with his drink, enough potassium cyanide to send him into convulsions and a coma within half an hour. They had even taken care of attire, so the Doreen walking beside him from bank to parking lot wore a discreet black linen dress with three-quarter sleeves. It was very different from the way she had started out this morning. "I can't go around in this," she had reasonably said, as they got into his car after breakfast.

He looked over at the pink eyelet. Even with Jane's sweater, it was not the sort of dress in which a widow talked to police detectives, turned aside the queries of reporters. "Don't you have a black one at home?"

"Martin didn't like me in black, he'd never let me get it."

"Then we'll have to buy one," he said, as though solving, for a weeping child, the most obvious of problems.

Compliant, agreeable to anything he suggested, she had
looked out the window. "Over there? Should I go in there?"
"There" was a store in the middle of the block; as he edged
into a parking place, the name obtruded. LAWSON'S. Was this
the one Jane had talked about: "The kids around here, they'll
walk into some place like Lawson's, pay those prices for some
little cotton to wear to school"? This store? Or a different
one? In any case, it hardly mattered, you couldn't propose
that someone in Doreen's situation start hunting for bargains.
The tearful eyes looked up at him. "I have—let's see—seven
dollars and twenty-five cents. No, here's another dime."
"You must have checks. Or they'll have a blank one."
"Martin said, just yesterday morning, Don't use the checking
account till I can—"
"Don't cry, Doreen. Of course I'll pay until—"
"You're so good to me."
Until you find out about the balance in your account, he
had intended to finish. But the grateful look had already
been turned on him: the ambiguity hovered, while he stood
outside under the green awning, was called in to write out
his own check—Lawson's, sixty-two fifty—received once again
her effusive thanks, drove off finally with the pink eyelet in
a box beside them. When they went to the bank, the temporary
nature of his contribution could be made clear.
However, now that they were coming from the bank, it
seemed less easy. She could pay, as a matter of fact: the
joint account of Martin and Doreen Cobden held $489.
"Doreen, if you want to make me out a check for that dress
now . . ." But when to say it? After the bank manager offered
his lugubrious handshake? While the documents bearing Martin's handwriting were confronting them? The moment for it
approached, slipped away, came into readiness, vanished again
—how talk about sixty-two fifty to one who had not yet faced
the fact that her husband's salary had permanently ceased,
this balance would not be automatically replenished next Tuesday or next month or even next year?
Indeed, the amount for a dress seemed minuscule compared

with the problems she was facing—problems it was incumbent on him to make clear to her, because who else was responsible? "Doreen, did Martin ever say anything about insurance?"

She looked toward the sky, as if the word might be floating there in some area just out of reach. "Insurance?"

"Was his life insured? He must have mentioned it."

"He always did the accounts. I didn't bother about money matters, it was his worry, he said."

"I see." He had a momentary vision of Jane: competent, cheerful, she would roll up the sleeves of her blue sweater and sit at the desk to do the income tax. "You ought to get some benefits out of marrying an Economics major," she would say. The desk lamp would shine on her face, which looked entirely composed as she glided along the numbered columns.

He spoke gently. "Even if he had insurance, there might be a no-liability clause. You'll have to look through the contract."

"You look, please. I never can read that official stuff."

"He'll have something in the retirement fund anyhow."

Again that upward look: mysterious, elusive, "retirement fund" was revolving up there with "insurance" and "liability." Then she smoothed down her dress as they waited to cross the street. It was a becoming dress, actually: its tailored lines and small round collar brought out a sweet seriousness in her small, even features. Now was the time to say it: If you want to pay me for the dress, Doreen . . .

"I could sell the boat," she said.

"What boat?"

"Our motorboat. I don't know what Martin paid, but he must have got it cheap because this Mr. Hollbrook was moving away in a hurry. And with prices going up all the time . . . well, wouldn't that amount to a lot?"

Doreen, you need money to live on. Money to pay the rent, buy groceries. Then he looked at her eager face. It was her first contribution, the first token of her own ability to plan. The profit over a distant and wholly conjectural purchase price seemed to her meaningful and heartening. "Of course, Doreen. Fine idea."

"And I can babysit a lot. Not for those Klempners, they don't have a penny, but lots of other families right there in the apartment."

The apartment which it must have taken plenty of tight planning to swing on Martin's salary. Suddenly he was furious. Not at Doreen, she couldn't help being impractical, but at Martin for making no provision, leaving a wife so unprotected, hoisting his problems onto the shoulders of others.

He took Doreen's arm as they crossed toward the car park. Ten twenty-five: he would just be giving the assignment at the end of third period. "Mr. Bassett, please postpone the composition till Thursday," Loretta Harris would beg. If anyone saw him crossing Maplemoor Street at this time of morning, they would wonder. If one of the PTA ladies saw him, for instance. Or a friend of Jane's. Or one of the students, missing school for the dentist. Then someone did see him. Or, at least, after the car went by and he had offered a perfunctory nod to its driver, he thought it must be Steve Slocum; on any morning, that dented tan fender was likely to be next to his in the school parking lot. It could well be Steve; as psychologist for both the junior and senior high schools, he drove frequently from one to the other.

He glanced at Doreen; she was looking thoughtfully after the tan car too. "You know Steve Slocum?"

"What? Oh, yes, I . . . that is . . ."

He opened the car door for her.

"Once Martin introduced me. That is, I don't really know him. . . ."

Her disquiet at seeing someone—anyone—from school reminded him of all the awkward moments he himself would have to face. Sooner or later, everyone on the faculty would find out what his own role in Martin's death had been. It was going to happen—whether he befriended Martin's wife or not. However, must it happen so soon? Must he run into just the faculty member whose stock-in-trade was indiscretion, who was the most proficient at finding out information about others and the most exuberant about passing it on?

"Or my fur coat from four years ago, I could sell that."

He stared: Doreen was back with the fantasy of her own economics.

"This darling seal, with mink collar—it was for our first anniversary. I was reading about this place, they give you top prices."

Sell the motorboat, the seal with mink collar—she still had not the faintest concept of anything.

"Only they cheat you in those places if you aren't careful."

"We'll see that they don't cheat you." When you thought about it, where was the harm? These little details sustained her, gave her a feeling of comfort and purpose. He couldn't at this moment bring her face to face with the reality of her own precarious state any more than he could remind her that he was out sixty-two fifty for that dress. He had handled things in the only way possible, he thought, when at three o'clock he finally left her and drove over to school. It was quiet: a few students still standing around on the steps, a few teachers working in their classrooms. Angie was locking hers, but she joined him as he walked along the hall.

"My God. What a thing to happen."

"Yes." They stood a minute in front of Martin's door. Just yesterday at this time, looking bored, slightly weary, Martin had gathered his papers and left with the promptness that surprised no one because it was years since he had devoted to school more hours than were strictly required.

Then they went on to Tony's room. Or not exactly his room: for the first time, a substitute had taken over. He stared, as though he could see some difference, but even his handwriting was still on the board from the day before: Lit. book, pages 83 to 97.

"I'll miss him like hell—you know that?" It was typical of Angie: a truculent aspect even to her grief. "This whole ridiculous high school will miss him. His being here raised the level—made it a little less ridiculous."

He nodded but said nothing. The windows were open from the bottom—that was a difference. In an effort to assert authority, substitutes generally made a big show of letting in fresh air, improving ventilation.

"He'd try to weasel out of jobs, or he'd go for days on end with that sour look on his face. But still, a very . . . civilized man."

Civilized—exactly. However, he still said nothing; there was nothing to say. Angie must have decided that too—though she was still walking around the room, her angular figure bumping into the sides of desks, her tone was determinedly casual. "That Mrs. Wesley who subbed for you today—they gave her a hard time fourth period, I heard it through the walls."

"They give me a hard time too." Mrs. Wesley's reports must be in his box in the office, along with announcements and class book: inattention and disruption of class work, it would euphemistically say.

"But otherwise not a sound, you have them in good shape." Angie turned, scraped her hips ungracefully against the blackboard, started up another row. "How come you were absent anyhow?"

"I thought I'd stay around with Martin's wife. Help her talk to the police. Make arrangements. That kind of thing."

"You're a sweet guy, Tony, I always said so. Especially since it's not a legal absence, you'll be docked for it." Angie shrugged her bony shoulders—then she sat facing him. "Listen. You might as well apply for that damn job now."

"What?"

"Department head. With Martin gone, you're certainly next in line. I mean, sentiment's fine, Tony, but right now you can't afford it. You have to get that application in right away."

He stared. She was entirely serious. She had no idea he had already applied. They had been good friends too long for her to dissemble, the last thing she would think of was sparing his feelings or evading the facts.

Furthermore, if Angie didn't know, no one else did either; her grasp of the faculty grapevine was more tenacious and experienced than anyone else's. No one else knew and no one else would find out, because who would tell them? Certainly not the principal, and even more certainly not the members of the Board of Education, because their aim was precisely to curtail gossip, eradicate unpleasantness, prevent any development that would impair the usefulness of teachers. Those accusations he had been expecting, those looks with the sly insinuations of blame . . . they would not be forthcoming.

"You can get it in by morning—one of your strong effective letters. Be a pushover—they'll vote you in at the meeting Thursday."

He rearranged the folders on his desk. "What about you?" he said jovially, conscious of the falseness.

"God, no. They resent me around here enough as is—bigmouth spinster. Imagine if I started bossing them around. Telling them how to teach linguistics. Asking for their lesson plans for next April. Besides, I have enough money."

"Lucky you."

"Damn lucky. No husband. No family. No dates to buy clothes for—who needs money?" She pulled at the twisted seam of a stocking. "But you with a baby, pretty wife who probably wants three more of them—Lord knows how you manage as is."

"Oh, well." The equivocal shrug may have satisfied her; she could go home to her solitary kitchen, her miniature steak, her lecture at the poetry club. He looked again around the room over which, for a day, someone else had presided. They would have been kept at spelling, that mainstay of the hardpressed substitute. Also, some busy work in the grammar books, maybe a tentative sortie into literature—"What's the turning point of this novel?" she would ask above the ungenerous snickers.

A sub in Martin's room also, he thought—someone else standing next to the torn posters, the overdue books. If things went well, speculation about Martin's death would be kept to a minimum. Why did he do it?—given any perspicacity on the part of a teacher, this question would be circumvented, discussion would plunge into the more suitable enigmas of *Wuthering Heights.*

Then he saw he might need to be perspicacious himself. "So you got here, Tony."

"Um-hmm." No reason Steve Slocum shouldn't stop, if he happened to be passing by. But why, just today, would he happen to pass by, when his office was on the third floor of another wing? "Come on in. Sit down."

Steve did sit, sliding with a neat sideways motion into one of the undersized desks. He had a knack for fitting in, looking at home in any situation. "Martin's room was right across the hall, wasn't it?"

"Yes."

"The poor bastard. I don't suppose you know any more than was in the papers."

"No."

"He ever give you any hint of depression? Melancholy?"

Nothing to reproach yourself for. Nothing. "He had his moods, I guess. Like the rest of us."

"Not that the hints mean anything, sometimes even the professionals miss all the signs." Steve rubbed his hand along the desk top. "The little I knew him, he was a very interesting guy."

"Yes. Wonderful."

"I guess we'll never figure why he did it."

No one has to figure, because I know. I took the job he'd been waiting for. I not only took it, I was so damn dumb I didn't realize when he told me how much he wanted it, needed it for his self-esteem. I pulled the chair out from under him. Me, his best friend around here. I'm the one with the whole story and the whole burden of reproach.

But no one knew all this—he must remember. No one would know unless Steve found out; Steve was the main person to guard against. Because while Steve was an expert counselor—the school was full of children he kept going—he was also an expert at turning the screw, making people squirm. He would never betray those secrets that came to him professionally,

but he had a professional's malevolent knowledge about finding out other secrets and using them. I tell you the joke about
the two homosexuals? he would ask a group that included
the gentle, effeminate Mr. Sloane. Or, there goes Mrs. Blanchard, longest menopause on record, he would say jovially to
a colleague of similar age as Mrs. Blanchard and even worse
irascibility. Or, I hear the new fellow in Chemistry is in the
market for a pretty wife, he would confide to Angie and
whatever others were walking with him across the parking lot.

Tony was conscious of Steve's scrutiny now. Had he guessed
anything? Was he already planning to move in for the attack?
"Didn't I see you with Martin's wife this morning?"

"I was helping her. Bank statements. Funeral arrangements."

"Very generous of you. Especially since it's not a legal
absence." The neat features turned sideways. "Or is it?"

"No." It was only in the school system that an exact mone-
tary value could be put on your generosity. In any other
profession, if you did a favor, your colleagues knew vaguely
it took you time, cost you money, put you to inconvenience.
But as a schoolteacher, the exact dimension of your sacrifice
went on record: thirty-one dollars and eighty cents subtracted
from next month's pay. This same silent computation had been
in Angie's eyes, and for all her cheerful fussing about hot
rolls at breakfast, it had dominated Jane's mind as she said
good-by this morning.

"Did you know Martin well? Were you good friends?"

Did he know Martin well. If he said No, the relentless in-
vestigator in Steve would look for another reason for Tony's
solicitude with Martin's wife. And having found it, he would
use it. Broadcast it. Consider it fair game. "Yes. Yes, we were."

"Friends outside school?"

He was in for it now. "Yes."

"Good friends for a long time?"

"I've only been here three years." He must not sound ir-
ritated. Something bothering you about this conversation?
Steve would ask. Is it rubbing you the wrong way?

"That poor Doreen—sweet little thing, isn't she?"

"Yes, she is."

"Terrible for her. Rotten." Steve was at the door. "Nice apartment they have now, I hope she can keep it, but remember that place they had on Rivers Street?"

There was not even time to consider. Rivers Street. In that small area between Melrose and the highway? Or was it further north, toward the shopping center? "Yes," he said. "Not nearly as nice."

"Well. See you." Inquisition over; he was alone at the window. Outside, trailing their hockey sticks along the spongy ground, girls with knee guards and jerseys headed back toward the gym. They walked easily—they must have won. He could feel easy too. Just because he wasn't used to lying, he never did it. . . . Besides, such a small lie: that he knew people when they lived in their former apartment. Small, irrelevant, insignificant—how could it possibly make a difference?

6

When she had read the letter, Jane looked, for a second, out the window. In the court below, children were playing without sweaters—it would be another hot day. Sitting in the playground with the babies, they would have to move into the shade. "I don't know about you," Linda would say, "but I'm definitely going to brush up on my French. We can't let our minds go to pot."

She picked up the letter again.

"Dear Classmate: I am writing to a very select few. If you are reading this letter, it means you were a VIP on campus, someone obviously slated for an exciting life. Please write us about it all. What interesting people do you meet? Which adventuresome places do you visit? We need news and more news for the alumni bulletin. . . ."

She threw the letter away and went in to Betsy, but the mid-morning sleep was under way, it could last for an hour. She could wash curtains or clean the medicine cabinet—which of these would numb her, keep her from brooding? Tony wouldn't brood, he would have no time. No matter how upset he was, he would have to give a vocabulary quiz in period four, and explain iambic pentameter in period five, and collect absence slips in homeroom. If melancholy settled, the twelve-twenty bell would disrupt it; if the image of Martin's gaze rose before him, the crowd of boys in the hallway would take precedence. He would not even have to decide what to do, the schedule imposed its own discipline, ministered its own comfort.

He couldn't be approached by a phone call either; she and

Tony had been kept apart by Doreen last night, and now other barriers were set up—was there another job in which a wife couldn't get through to her husband, in the importunate tone that fooled no one start with some irrelevant reminder, then wait for the loving assurance which at that moment was essential? You could interrupt a man at a board meeting, a staff conference, a legal session, but if Jane Bassett felt cut off from her husband, she had to stay that way until late afternoon.

And even then accessibility did not lead to the endearments that were needed because within five minutes they were back on the same subject. "You mean she has no money at all?"

"Practically none. About five hundred dollars in their checking account and another couple of hundred in some savings bank. But that's the whole story. No insurance. No holdings salted away."

She took off her apron. "Doreen's family—can't they help?"

"You heard. Her father dead, her mother in a rest home—I think Martin had been giving money there."

She put cheese and crackers beside his drink. "What about Martin's family?"

"Due in tonight, thank goodness—a brother and his wife."

"Well, he'd been teaching seventeen years, if he put in the minimum he must have . . . let's see . . . three thousand eight hundred and fifty dollars in the retirement fund."

"Exactly." He was looking at her with the familiar expression of doubtful surprise: it never ceased to amaze him when she summoned up columns of figures in her mind and maneuvered effortlessly through them. Tony could not understand that percentages, decimals, equations would wear the same friendly aspect for some people that a Shakespeare sonnet had for him. Even in college, her skills had confounded him; "A pretty Economics major," he said in amazement when they first met, as if it were a contradiction in terms, the mathematical mind must exclude the feminine appeal—for a smart man, he was in this regard curiously old-fashioned.

"What's Doreen planning to do?"

"She doesn't realize she has to plan anything. She says she'll give herself permanents, use margarine instead of butter."

"You mean, she thinks she can go on living in that apartment? This crazy suburb?"

"It hasn't penetrated that she might not be able to." His tone, however, was indulgent; Doreen's impractical outlook was a matter for tolerant acceptance.

"Well, she better face the facts pretty soon," Jane said briskly. And when Tony didn't answer—"I mean, you can't keep someone living in a dream world."

"You also can't pound economics down their throat the day after their husband dies."

She was the callous type who wanted to pound economics —was that what he meant? Anger rose in her—then she remembered how tired he must be. "Tony, it's for her sake. When every penny is cutting into her tiny capital."

He picked up a cracker, put cheese on it, laid it down.

"And she can count on us for friendship and advice, she's entitled to that, but she must know that no other teacher can help her out on the money end. Mustn't she?" she added with a little laugh—he still had that abstracted look.

"Well, I—"

"Tony, we can't give her money. We simply can't. I mean, it's bad enough you're teaching."

"Bad enough?"

All right, you said it now. You can't change it. You have to brazen it out. "Darling, I meant bad enough for someone brilliant like you to make eight thousand, when people with half your brains—"

"We decided on this together, Jane. I explained all the disadvantages. We discussed it."

"I didn't mean—"

"Maybe we should open the discussion again."

"Tony, have something to eat."

"I can still switch. I have that offer."

"What offer?" she couldn't stop herself from saying.

"McHenry still would take me, I'm sure of it."

For a second her blood raced. It had happened last fall: a father who spotted Tony at back-to-school night, heard him speak, called the next day to make the offer. Vice president in charge of sales for a linoleum company. Twenty thousand a year to start. On twenty thousand—how often the thoughts had crept in—you could live in a house, and buy a sleeveless linen dress just because you liked it, and be part of that easy-going social life that was reported nightly in the *Stoneycrest Chronicle.*

Then she saw his face. "Tony, we talked it over years ago, it's settled. You're doing what you love. . . ."

"Bad enough you're teaching."

"It slipped out. I never said it."

"Linoleum is very big now. This new promotional campaign."

She edged toward the kitchen; she had to test the string beans.

"Bad enough you're—"

"Tony darling, forget it. I beg you."

She bent over the stove. Sales manager. Twenty thousand . . . no ideas for two people to be talking about on a day when the washing machine broke, Betsy had heat rash, the two of them were distraught. The two of them were distraught because of the problem they were not mentioning, she had put off mentioning. But for how long must she put it off? When would there be a time when wifely lure and strategic readiness were in there working for her?

"Tony, listen. The two of us squabbling . . . if you didn't have all those wrong ideas we wouldn't do it."

"Wrong ideas about what?"

"About Martin, of course. Committing suicide." He was listening so intently that she took heart, she went on. "I mean, for years you've said Martin was evasive, no one could understand him. But here you are . . . you and everyone else . . . jumping to the conclusion you understand this."

For a second he leaned toward her—only a second. "Jane, it's no use. I've thought and thought—if there were a shred of evidence in some other direction. But the straight fact is Martin expected that job. Counted on it. Besides," he went on in the labored voice that was so unnatural to him, alien to his boyish good looks, "even if there were other causes and the job triggered it, don't you see, Jane, I'm still to blame?"

She had said all the wrong things earlier, and now this talk was simply compounding his misery. Was it her fault? If she were smarter, could she reach him?

"If the police are satisfied, I don't see why you—"

"Who says they're satisfied," she burst out. " 'The police have tentatively accepted the theory of suicide'—that's what the papers said this morning, and it doesn't sound satisfied in the least. It sounds evasive, like someone not looking for expense or trouble. An insignificant schoolteacher swallows poison—it could very well be suicide, it has lots of elements of suicide, why investigate further? Investigations can make trouble—instead of a case sewed up, there's another of the files marked *Incomplete.*"

"What about that letter?"

"There could be other explanations for that too. . . . No, I don't have any. There just could be, is all I'm saying. If someone would take the pains to look. And if you weren't so wrapped up in your own guilt."

"Jane, what's your theory?" he said.

She spoke slowly, against the trembling. "There was some other element in Martin's death. He was a frustrated man, and he was disappointed about a job, but there's more to it than that. Something we don't know. Something that would change the whole picture if we could grab hold of it. Tony, don't you agree?"

He didn't agree, but he might: there was an incipient softness in his face. As she went in to change Betsy, she thought, after dinner she would try again, they would slip into that state whereby each appropriated the ideas of the other. If we could just be alone, she thought, as the phone rang, and Tony picked it up, and she knew before he had said a word that they were in for it again.

"That was Doreen."

"I figured."

"Martin's brother just phoned. They aren't coming after all —that expensive fare from California."

She folded a diaper over Betsy's fat legs.

"So she's having the funeral at four tomorrow, no point waiting."

"I see."

"She'd been calm when I left. Thinking relatives were coming, having that to look forward to."

She knew from the pucker on Betsy's face that she must have made a sudden spasmodic motion.

"But now, just facing the evening alone in that apartment."

"She has no other friends?"

"Evidently not." His eyes were fixed on the wall; that spectacle he usually loved, Betsy waving her ridiculous toes while someone tried to hold her, had no power to delight him. "Jane, you can stretch it, can't you? Whatever we have for supper."

"It's veal scallopini." It was not, in fact, stretchable at all; you had to know to a penny the size of the package that would do for the two of them. And while Tony knew all this too— Live dangerously, darling, he would tell her when they went marketing together—of course he couldn't be expected to think about it now: Doreen definitely could not be left weeping alone in an apartment.

"Of course there's plenty," she said when Doreen finally appeared, looking surprisingly pretty in a black linen dress. The dress gave an unaccustomed dignity to her round face—much better than yesterday's pink eyelet. How nice you look, Doreen, she wanted to say, and realized its inappropriateness.

"I'm sorry about Martin's brother," she said instead.

"All that way, California and back, it really is inconvenient."

"Maybe they'll come later," she said consolingly—then, hearing Doreen murmur placidly about the long trip, the expense, she understood this particular consolation was not needed at all. Doreen's feelings did not go deep enough to be hurt—

accommodating, flexible, pliant, they would bend with events, sway as circumstances blew them.

"You're both so wonderful, letting me come at the last minute like this."

"We wanted you," she said stanchly.

"I don't care a bit what I eat, just a sandwich, any old thing."

"I told you. Plenty," she said, and pulled a lettuce leaf over her own bare plate. The plates lay close on the small table—the three of them here in front of the window were by now a pattern, a unit.

"Martin's brother—do you know them well?"

"They visited twice. Once last year, but they had all these theater tickets. And the other time was four years ago, just after we were married."

"Was it when you lived on Rivers Street?" Tony unexpectedly asked.

"Rivers Street. Down near Elm, you mean that one?"

"I guess so."

"Oh, well, we didn't live there anyhow. We never lived anyplace else—we moved into this apartment right away, it's so nice we stayed and stayed."

"I thought you were there," he murmured, and his voice was so unsteady that she looked at him sharply. How pale he was—almost gray. Oh, my darling, she thought, I've been so awful, I've made things worse.

"What kind of accident was there, before you and Martin got married?" she surprised herself by asking.

"We were mountain climbing. I used to be terrified—all those rocky peaks. But Martin said you couldn't miss a view, not a single one."

"You mean, he fell?"

"Oh, no," Doreen said brightly. "I was the one. But Martin was wonderful, he really was. He just stayed up there the whole time. All summer long, till I got better. And I'm practically perfect now, you mustn't feel sorry for me a bit." Her brave smile went across the table. "Let me help you with the dishes."

"Nothing much. Just fruit for dessert." She spoke absently, gathering the plates.

"I want to help. When I think of all you've done."

"Nothing," she said again.

"Oh, but it is. For Tony to take a whole day off and come around with me and buy me this dress at Lawson's and everything, please let me help."

She felt smothered, she could hardly breathe—though her imagination gave her an exact picture of the pained look that must be twisting Tony's face, she kept her gaze on the table. There was a moment's silence; it hung in the small room, impaling them. Then Betsy began to cry.

"I'll get it. You stay here."

She stood next to the crib. A dress at Lawson's. Sometimes you could pick up something at Lawson's for forty or forty-five dollars, but most of their stock started at fifty and went on from there. Once, walking by with the carriage, she had priced a green cotton in the window; "Sixty-nine fifty, madam," the disinterested salesgirl had said. Say fifty dollars then—fifty dollars that Tony had forked over and decided not to mention. For fifty dollars she could cover the couch. Buy a decent vacuum. Treat herself to the tweed suit which for two years she had coveted. She stared at the closet, as if the suit were hanging there, between her corduroy bathrobe and her printed silk. Then Betsy cried once more; she had wriggled herself sideways across the crib.

Jane bent down. "For God's sake stay under the blanket," she shouted at the child.

7

Bad enough you're teaching. Bad. Bad enough. . . . She didn't mean it, Tony thought. She had said it without thinking. She had no desire for him to be one of those men who focused on sales figures and margins. She wouldn't let him do something he hated just so they could have an extra ten thousand dollars a year.

But however he went over it—however he had gone over it for two weeks—the memory of Jane's words still had the power to unsettle him. He stood at the window, watching the boys in gym uniform saunter out to after-school practice. Why was she being so difficult? Why, indeed, must his responsibility toward Doreen bring on that taut look, as though there were some way he could evade or diminish it? The fact was, Jane ought to be pleased: despite her inexperience, Doreen was doing all right, she was starting to make money. Though baking pies in her own kitchen had sounded unrealistic when first she proposed it, she had sized up Stoneycrest right: plenty of women would pay exorbitant prices for a good homemade dessert. They would not only pay; they would call each other up, they would rave about lemon chiffon and old-fashioned apple, they would lean across a bridge table to say how much better this little Mrs. Cobden did than their own Swedish cook. Doreen was now busy six days a week—when Tony stopped at her apartment after school, he found her in a bright confusion of sugar, strainers, mixing bowls, address books, fruit.

"Mrs. Lanihan just called. Twelve for dinner tomorrow night, she wants that coconut pie I made last Tuesday. Two of them." She was pouring cherries through a sieve; above it, her face was flushed.

"That's fine."

"And her friend Mrs. Knoll—no, don't sit there, oven's too hot. Over here, by the window."

He sat obediently, watching her blue and yellow apron swish around a table.

"And these people called Cassin, something for out-of-town-ers, so I'm trying something new. This cherry. . . . Here. Taste."

As he licked the spoon, he thought this was one time Jane's instincts had been wrong. "It just won't work, Tony." She had spoken with her usual composed practicality. "That image of the little woman in the kitchen—appealing, but not for today's world. She'll scrape snips of dough out of pans, and worry about a quarter of a pound of butter, and knock herself out with ideas for leftovers—and in the end they'll still go to that French pastry shop where twenty chefs are making icing."

Well, for once Jane had misread the signs. Because here was Doreen, getting orders like crazy and filling them. A timer rang, and she bent to open the oven. "For the Hammers downstairs. It's his sixtieth birthday—such a nice man, really, she's having a surprise party." A smudge of flour was on her face, red stains ran down her apron, the ribbon in her hair was undone, and she looked entirely content as she put the pies on a rack. "I took in seventy-eight dollars last week, you'll see when you add it up."

"Sounds about right."

"So that's forty dollars profit, at least. That is, if you don't count the thirty-six dollars I spent last night on a new mixer, but that's a long-term investment, isn't it? It really doesn't count."

He sighed; they had talked about her old mixer last week, agreed that with minor repairs it ought to hold up for another few months anyhow.

"Was it wrong?" Her contrite face turned toward him. "The

man said five dollars to fix the old one and then no guarantee or anything."

"Well—"

"When you think how long this new one will last, I really had to buy it, didn't I?"

"I guess you did, Doreen." He took another bite of the cherry filling. "Should we go over those books now?"

"Thing is, that boy from downstairs called, he can't do deliveries tonight. So I'm in trouble. Four lemon meringues, four different places. And a taxi would use up every bit of profit, all my hard afternoon for nothing."

"Of course you can't have your work go for nothing." He looked at his watch: twenty to six. Jane rushed to have the baby fed and bathed so he could play with her before dinner —in the half hour presided over by Betsy's crowing, an amity could be established that could take them through the evening, restore, conceivably, the equilibrium there had been until three weeks ago.

"Sure it's all right?" Doreen looked up at him.

"Fine. Plenty of—no, let me carry them." He carried them gingerly, conscious of the frailty of stiff icing, soft filling, flaky crust. However, she smiled with pleasure: the pies would be fine, he shouldn't worry a bit. If you didn't worry, things always turned out. Look at today. That boy calling at the last minute that he couldn't come, and here she was having the stuff delivered and getting this nice ride herself down Woodbine, which was her absolute favorite of all the beautiful streets in Stoneycrest. It was typical of everything about this business, she just loved it.

"It's the way lots of big businesses start, isn't it? Someone alone in her kitchen?"

"You won't want anything big for a long time, Doreen."

But everyone had been so nice, he couldn't believe how nice they were. Sometimes they talked to her when she was taking orders; they were not high hat at all. That Mrs. Andrews —right through those trees he could see the entrance. And Mrs. Battista, and that pretty Mrs. Lang—just because they had these big houses with enormous grounds didn't make them snooty or anything.

Then a customer turned up who was not so nice at all. Or rather, the friend of a customer, and nothing in the set-up to hint at unpleasantness beforehand. It was their last stop: the standard circular driveway, expanses of lawn, imposing entrance—he waited in the car while Doreen rang.

"Oh, Mrs. Cobden, so good of you. . . . Yes, I'll be careful, in the refrigerator this minute." Then the woman turned; from his seat behind the wheel, he could just see another face appear under the fan-shaped doorway.

"Mary, this is Mrs. Cobden, she bakes the most delicious pies. Mrs. Cobden, my friend Mrs. Merimee, some day we must get her to try one of your—"

"One of her what?" At the unexpected iciness in the second woman's voice, he looked up.

"Well, coconut is good, I had it last week, but the one I like best is still—"

"Thanks, dear. I'd rather keep charity out of the kitchen, if it's all the same to you."

"Mary, you're wrong, the quality really is—" However, the door was closed; a second later, Doreen was beside him.

"Some of them make it difficult. I'm sorry."

"It's nothing," she said.

"That woman—"

"Most of them are just darling, I honestly like doing it."

He drove out to the shaded street. "There was a Merimee boy in Martin's class last year. Bert. Bright kid, but in lots of trouble. I'm almost sure that was his mother, that good-looking face isn't one you forget."

"Doesn't matter," she said again.

"But Martin took a particular interest in this boy. Worked with him. Spent a lot of time with him. He used to tell me . . ." His voice trailed off. Standing next to the torn posters, the scratched desks, Martin used to tell him, but did that mean he, therefore, knew? He could be sure? If Martin had been so wonderful to the boy, why should the boy's mother go so conspicuously out of her way to be rude to Martin's widow? A sense of the number of unprovable facts about Martin came over him—that sense Jane had felt from the beginning and tried to impart to him. His own responsibility was unchanged —heavy, debilitating, it attended him—but around it there were all the details that themselves kept changing, shifting, blurring the outline of the man who drank Campari laced with cyanide at a kitchen table.

8

She looked in at the store window and then walked faster—she had to get her marketing done before it started to rain. No: she had to get her marketing expertly done, because good food had to make up for some notable other pleasures that were lacking between her and Tony these days.

The argument last night had been worse than usual. "You could have told me you were going to be late." . . . her implacable voice, to start things off when he got home.

"You knew I was going over to help Doreen, I told you."

"You didn't tell me you'd help her till twenty to seven."

"The fellow who drives for her got sick, I had to take one pie all the way to Oak and Laurel."

"Sounds dandy—my husband a delivery boy for Doreen."

He moved abruptly away. "Can I please see Betsy?"

"I bathed her at five-thirty so she'd be ready. She was tired and I made her stay up."

"I'll go in this minute."

"Be a great help. She just fell asleep."

"Jane, for heaven's sake, let's eat then."

"It's stew. When Betsy was crying so much, I let it stick to the pot."

Some of his papers fell off the desk, but he didn't try to pick them up. "We'll eat what's on top."

"Tastes awful, I just tried it."

"Jane, I have to help her, you know that. We've gone all over it."

"You mean, you've gone over it. You've decided to drown happily in your own guilt."

But though the taunt came out sharper than she had intended, his answering expression was bemused, almost speculative, rather than the expected angry one. "Jane, listen. She doesn't have an easy time. That is, things are mixed up. Confused. At one place we went to—"

"That poor Doreen, I know just how brave she is. How about another dress at Lawson's to reward all that noble bravery?"

"Certainly a pleasure to talk to you, you're always so sweet and understanding."

They had done it again: slipped into estrangement. However a conversation started out, it would wind up in that state where argument demeans itself as anger, persuasion comes out in accents of unserviceable fury. He was now as frigid as she was, but she had the feeling—the transitory feeling—that before she went in for that tired remark about the dress, he had been about to change the whole course of the conversation. She knew suddenly the ache of depression. Can't we handle anything, she thought. Is our marriage so frail it can't manage any complications at all? Other young people ran into trouble: dependent parents, job threats, illness. All she and Tony had was this silly Doreen—couldn't they surmount it?

She watched as he stood at last, stiffly, beside the window. If he would put his arms around me, she thought. That minute, while the rice turned soggy, the stew that neither of them cared about sank more thickly toward the bottom. But the fights these days were different. They caused none of those outbursts where you wounded someone, hurled the insults possible only toward one fully known and highly vulnerable, but they didn't head for any sweetly comforting epilogue either. Privacy and closeness—maybe they lost their potency after three years of marriage, you became impervious to them.

She would not accept that. She simply would not accept that. She framed a smile, as though already setting in front of him the delectable supper with which she would woo her husband tonight. An answering smile responded to her efforts, applauded them. However, it was not Tony's smile, it belonged to someone else—simultaneous with seeing it, she felt her hands clasped, her shoulders hugged, her face pressed next to another. "It really is—my darling Jane."

"Hello, Alan."

"Let me see—did this damn suburb spoil you? Turn this way. . . . No, little more."

"Alan. We're holding up traffic."

"No damage. You're still the prettiest thing south of Bridgeport."

"You're still the best talker."

"Come have a drink."

"Alan, I can't."

"It's respectable, I swear. Even on these innocent streets, a married woman is allowed to hold hands with an old classmate."

They were right back in the old affection. As she sat opposite him presently, in the bar of the Standish Arms, they weren't simply having an afternoon drink, they were adding one more to the chain of dates that had stretched across four years. The walks along a snowy campus, the parties after the parties after the prom, the talks that managed to be intimate despite the noise from the rest of the fraternity house—the proprietary gaze he turned on her evoked them all, was justified by them.

"Tell me everything. One baby or two?"

"One. All we can afford."

"How's the good-looking schoolteacher?"

"Listen, he didn't choose teaching as a last resort—I mean, he wasn't desperate or anything. He had lots of careers to choose from. Right now there's a job in linoleum. . . ." Then the sense of his quizzical look or her defensive tone came over her. "Tony. Well, he's wonderful."

"If he's so wonderful, why does he let you walk around in those frumpy clothes?"

"I'm not on parade. I'm out to buy round steak and mushrooms."

"Three years ago you wouldn't appear on East campus in a skirt that fit like that."

"Alan, you haven't changed a bit."

"Yes, I have. I'm more strong-minded now. Determined. I wouldn't make the same mistake again."

She was not going to ask him which mistake. Though she felt the solemn import of his look, from a face which was only inches away from her own, she was not going to ask or give him a chance to tell. She put down her glass with a little laugh. "I'm not used to drinking highballs at three in the afternoon."

"What are you used to doing?"

"Sitting in the playground."

"You just sit there? All afternoon?"

"Oh, we talk. Me and Linda and the others."

"Talk about what?"

"Which of the strained desserts is better. When can you expect them to start crawling. How long will they stay in the playpen."

"I'm certainly glad you were voted Spring Festival Queen our senior year."

She kept her eyes on the black-and-silver wallpaper—she'd been passing this place for three years, and she'd never known the way it looked inside. "What are you doing with yourself, Alan?"

"Right now, getting over a divorce."

"I'm sorry."

"Don't be. She wasn't for me—I knew that all the time. But she was fine for six months, which was what I wanted. And I can easily afford the alimony, which was what she wanted." He looked at her sideways. "Some great conveniences about the brokerage business, despite all your disapproval."

"I didn't disapprove. I just thought it was—"

"Sordid. Crass. I remember. Guess how much that sordid business grossed last year."

"Alan, I don't even think in big numbers any more. What I read is mostly the print on cans of peas. Which is the best buy for thirty-two cents." Then, hearing the note of self-pity, disavowing it, she finished her drink. "Do you like the business?"

"I'm damn good at it," he said. "I have lots of useful attributes. I guess I always had them, but I didn't realize. For instance, I'm persuasive. I can get what I really put my mind to."

She turned the glass around in her fingers.

"That was my big mistake—don't you think you can get me not to say it—not arguing with you. You had this dumb idea about marriage, really, darling, for a smart girl you were terribly dumb, and I let you get away with it. I didn't talk you out of that idiotic stand."

She turned the glass faster. Should she say his assumption was unwarranted, that however persistent his arguments, they would not have altered anything? She followed his gaze to a point between their hands, as though the assumption were lying there, solid, immutable, on the table top. Was it true? Untrue? By not contradicting it, was she in effect admitting its veracity? Or would a contradiction simply raise it in importance, make something memorable and significant out of this light-hearted moment between old friends?

At the same time, however, she thought: whoever did respond to his persuasiveness would be lucky. He would certainly have another wife, he was too attractive to stay alone for very long, and the girl would have a fine time. There would always be interesting people. There would be the kind of parties written up in the newspapers with those gayly cryptic allusions that defeated any outsider. There would be an unending cycle of stylish events, so it wouldn't be in the least unusual to come into a bar like this and sit having a drink in mid-afternoon. It all would add up: someone married to Alan would know exactly who she was, what to do, how to operate.

That girl . . . Alan's wife . . . for a second she trembled with vividness. Did Alan understand that? Was it why he leaned forward with that intense look? However, he had always been tactful, too—he was a darling in that direction. "Nice place, Stoneycrest. You're lucky to live here."

"Certainly is beautiful. Gorgeous." Much better, she thought, hearing the safe impersonality of her voice. Keep it like this.

"Fine waterfront, too. All those places where you go right across the lawn and onto the dock."

"Very convenient," she murmured, and paused while he ordered another drink. Should she object? Was it time to think of leaving? She felt her smile go out to include Alan, the waiter, even the girl in the yellow dress at the next table. "What are you doing here?"

"I took a couple of days off. I have cousins—second cousins, really—with a yacht."

Of course Alan would have cousins with a yacht in Stoneycrest—if she'd been living in San Francisco or Rome, he would have turned up with relatives there as well. He had always had a crew of great uncles, brothers-in-law, cousins, toward all of whom he had the warmest feelings and from all of whom he was able to get help in expediting his generous impulses. He wouldn't brag about these relatives, it was nothing like that, it just happened that there would be a moment when it was suitable for him to murmur about his uncle the judge, or the producer, or the retired general. "Trouble with that visa?" he would say to a distraught roommate. "Why don't I mention it to my aunt's husband, he was just appointed ambassador down there, we're playing tennis next Thursday." Or, "Why didn't you tell me about these delays? My brother-in-law is head of the agency, once he takes a look at the plans . . ." And though his voice emphasized that it had nothing to do with him, just an accident that his sister had married the one fellow in the State Department who could help—despite these tacit disclaimers, Alan had seemed solid, dependable, even before he was twenty: you knew you could count on him.

"My cousins live on Woodbine Street. The Everetts. Maybe you know them."

"Don't think I do."

"Martha and Les."

"Doesn't ring a bell."

"You'd like them, Jane. Little older than you, five, six years, but you'd have a lot in common."

She put down her glass; it was empty, she saw in surprise. "Alan, you don't understand. I mean, you just couldn't be more wrong." She giggled a little; for all that knowledgeability, Alan certainly did have some quaint ideas. "The chance of my being friends with people on Woodbine—it just isn't in the cards. They live half a mile away, but that's also worlds away. Understand, Alan?—worlds." She knew she was talking too much, or too fast, or with too great an air of cozy confidence, but it could not matter. This was her old friend Alan; he used to take her books back to the library, comfort her before she had to take a test—she could say anything to a friend like Alan, couldn't she?

"Those cousins of yours—they must be terribly rich or they wouldn't live there. And we—we're not poor, heavens, I'm not saying that. But next to them. I mean, compared to all of them. Listen." She leaned forward, one imparting the jolliest of secrets. "How many do they have in help?"

"Janey, I haven't even—"

"Three, let's say. Four. The butler makes more than Tony. And Mrs. Everett—I happen to know she picks up any old thing in Lawson's just to putter around in the garden. Lawson's. Well, it's this little store, we live right around the corner, in an apartment. In Stoneycrest they think it's a good idea to have some apartments, it gives the place—what's the word? —diversity."

He was looking at her judiciously. Had she said too much— for a second she couldn't remember what they had been talking about. "I'm glad life isn't so austere that you can't get out once in a while," he said primly.

"I'm not exactly out. I mean, from one to two I watched Linda's child so she could market, now she's watching mine."

"Get her for tomorrow," he said suddenly. "Tell her you'll

watch hers next Tuesday. While she shops for—what does Linda need?"

"Bedspreads." She giggled again—now she knew she must be a little drunk.

"Fine. New bedspreads for Linda."

"You want me to go on a yacht with your cousins on Woodbine?"

"No, Janey love." He reached over briefly to take her hand. "I want you to come off with me alone. Some place in the country."

"Alan, you're a darling, but it's impossible."

"Just the kind of change you need. We'll find some nice restaurant. Maybe I'll buy you a new dress."

"I shouldn't have said all that. Please forget it."

"But it's for me, Janey. To give me pleasure. What you don't realize, men like to do things for women. Like taking care of them. Being responsible for them. It makes us feel—well, masterful. Protective. . . . Janey. Anything wrong?"

She was sitting very straight; suddenly the euphoric haze was quite gone. "Being responsible for them . . ."

"Satisfies our masculine vanity. Does us good."

"Alan, listen. I would like to go riding in the country. I just realized."

He sat silent, watching her.

"But it's a business trip, sort of. I mean, there's this little hotel—or maybe there isn't, that's what I have to see. It's on the Appalachian Trail, in a place called Harrod. Harrod, Vermont. If you wouldn't mind driving all the way up . . ."

"Eight-thirty tomorrow, Janey. We set out for Harrod, Vermont."

9

"It might be a wild-goose chase."

"Janey, such a beautiful day, sit back and relax."

"If I don't find out anything. If we waste the whole time."

"Nothing's a waste if I'm sitting next to you, we're driving together."

"If only I could catch her definitely in a lie. This girl . . . Doreen . . ."

"Nice girl?"

"Terrible, that's the point. A little sneak . . . at least, I have this idea she's a little sneak."

"Since she's so terrible, let's not talk about her."

They might suspend talk, but the insidious thoughts would persist. Because Doreen was persisting, exacting the tribute about which Tony now felt masterful, protective, but might not if there were proof that she . . . if there were proof . . .

"I don't even know what I'm going to look for."

"Janey, love, you said it was your own business. Private—you didn't want to talk about it. Correct? We agreed when we left your house and again at Hartford, and here it is past Springfield and—"

"Alan, you're a darling."

"That's the way." He reached over to pat her knee. "We're in a good car. The weather's fine. We're getting sunburned. Any time I want I can see a pretty profile, which happens to be my favorite view. Okay? We leave it like that?"

She nodded, though it didn't work out exactly like that—the worry was undiminished. "We'll have to stop when we get to Harrod. Get some maps."

"I have the maps." He reached into a pocket. "Here. Appalachian Trail. Also, this detailed map of lower Vermont in case—"

"Alan, do you always think of everything? Go to endless bother?"

"No bother, I just ordered it."

He said it in the usual offhand way, but she had a sense of all the favors he could deliver, all the bequests that would always be at his power to give. A map of the Appalachian Trail, an introduction to the head of some strategic agency, a day off to drive to Vermont whenever a girl needed it . . . with Alan it would all be easy.

He would also understand about whatever urgency churned inside someone else. "Couple of nice places on the way, but I thought we wouldn't stop. That hotel—they'll answer questions better if you plunk down three-fifty for the Tuesday lunch special."

"I can never begin to thank—"

"Quit biting your nails, Janey, we'll be there in less than an hour." And he was right about this too, of course, because at the next exit he turned off the highway, chose from the mental map that had been inscribed beforehand the correct one of the three available asphalt roads, turned right presently on the two-lane road where a sign marked CONSTRUCTION meant only that some sand had been dumped along one shoulder, evaded some serious holes made by recent rainstorms, and pulled up, at the time assigned, in the dirt-covered area which was a parking lot for the Alpine Gap Motel.

She stared at the long porch, the uncertain collection of cottages that gradually took shape behind the trees. "You're sure this is it?"

"Only hotel on the Trail—don't you like it?"

"I guess so." But the disappointment hovered—had she been expecting to catch Doreen in some massive lie, some fiction which would reveal all that was hidden behind that seemingly aimless chatter? Here, unmistakably, was a hotel, and there looming behind it was a mountain—a small-size mountain,

but a mountain, nonetheless—and tacked to that conspicuous
tree trunk was a sign which, like all signs saluting hardy walk-
ers from Florida to Maine, computed mileage to the nearest
shelter. At the desk inside, a man came slowly; he was not
expecting visitors; he peered without interest across the counter
where dust had settled on the samples of hand-woven baskets,
the boxes of maple sugar candy. Lunch? Well, yes, he reckoned they could have lunch. The ladies' bridge club from
East Farmingdale was meeting and maybe some directors from
the bank, but there certainly would be room for two more,
right in there—they should go right in.

"Thanks very much. See you at the table, Janey." Alan went
off—once more he was smoothing the way, making it easy. She
leaned an elbow on the counter.

"A friend of mine told me to be sure to come here." The
man nodded: one who could take testimonials or leave them.

"Doreen. I don't know what her last name was." Alan would
know; Alan would have had the sense to find out, or get someone else to find out. "Not a guest here, actually, she used to
work here."

But he shook his head. They never had any Doreen.

"It must have been four, five years ago. Maybe you
weren't—"

"Been here twelve years. Seen lots of them come and go,
but no Doreen."

She stood in indecision. Would it fizzle out like this, at a
desk with the wicker baskets, the boxes open on top to show
the tan squares of candy. "She married a schoolteacher who
used to come here. Martin Cobden."

Mr. Cobden—why didn't she say so at the beginning. Mr.
Cobden certainly did like to come up.

"He's—dead. He died three weeks ago."

The man sighed. He was sorry to hear that, he really was.
If there was a nicer man than Mr. Cobden. And how he loved
the mountains. That mountain back there—no, through this
side window she could see it—whatever the weather, he'd put
on his hiking shoes and that old blue jacket and go up.

"That's what she told us. Doreen."

He looked at her sourly. "You mean Doris, why didn't you say so?"

"Doris?"

"Her rightful name. What I say is, people have a name, they ought to stick to it, what kind of world if everyone shifted their name whichever way every two minutes."

When the door opened behind her, four ladies in straw hats and printed dresses walked past—Alan would have the East Farmingdale Bridge Club for company. "She changed her name to Doreen?"

"I don't rightly know what she changed it to. Never wanted to know. Doris, fresh linens for 38—what I used to say to her. Doris, the morning newspaper for Mr. Langer. Doris, wear decent shoes, you'll go breaking your neck with those sandals."

She offered an equivocal smile. "Doreen—Doris—she told me she met Mr. Cobden while she was working behind the desk."

"Work . . . all those girls who say they'll do anything. But they can't type, and they won't make beds, and ask them to help out in the kitchen, you'd think a mortal insult." He rearranged the sign in front of the baskets: $2.95 TO $6.95 FOR BEAUTIFUL HANDMADE WORK. "But she wasn't so dumb, I'll say that. She could spot a nice man when she saw him. She could manage so she'd be waiting down here when he came out of the dining room, she could manage that all right."

Was that all? Doreen had aspired to a name with pretensions to elegance, she had contrived, like any girl, to display her availability when an unattached man was around—was that what she and Alan had come all the way to find out? She waited while the man answered the phone, said he reckoned there might be a room a week from Wednesday. "Terrible about that accident," she murmured then.

"I warned her, she'll be the first to admit it. Like I told you."

"Told me what?"

"Those damn fool sandals," he said, and turned to go back to the office.

She stood trembling. He must not leave. He must keep stand-

ing here, feeling the conviction of superior insights, receiving
the credit for calling the shots. "If only Doreen had listened
to you," she said.

"Sensible advice, but would she follow it? I even called
after her. Doris, you know those rocks stay slippery for days
after a rain—just what I told her. Doris, you'll be sorry."

She saw her hands tight on the edge of the counter. "What
about Mr. Cobden. Didn't he hear?"

"Probably halfway up the mountain by then. And all right
to go chasing after him, plenty of girls these days. But not in
those sandals. Not looking for trouble on a slippery trail."

"You're so right. You're so absolutely right." Asking for
trouble. She looked inside, past a rustic doorway. At a table
by a window, Alan would be studying the menu, pretending
not to hear the talk of the bridge ladies. "Was it a bad fall?"

"Bad enough so she lay there half dead. Leastwise from his
face when he rushed down for help, you'd think she was half
dead. And then till they got her on a stretcher, brought her
down—any man would be crazy."

"It really wasn't fair, was it?" she said, and knew even before
he answered he must misunderstand.

"No fun for your little friend, I grant you. But if she'd took
my advice."

"Yes." She didn't have to worry about his stopping now—
on the grounds of having almost forestalled an accident, he
had appropriated it, built himself into it. The unheeded advice flickered with a life of its own, warming his spirits, sus-
taining any conversation that would pay it tribute.

"And that poor Mr. Cobden—almost worse for him. The way
he worried himself sick. Walked around here thinking it was
his fault."

Was it over by that window Martin had stood with his
somber thoughts, his guilt-stricken face? Next to the fireplace?
Or had he climbed the mountain again, surveyed the rock
down which a girl looking for trouble had slid in her ill-
advised, her deliberately worn sandals?

Then Doreen's voice came back: Practically perfect, you

don't have to feel sorry for me. . . . "I never asked her. I hope the accident didn't leave her with any damage."

The man made another stab at the baskets. He wouldn't know about damage, things like that. But to see the long face Mr. Cobden was wearing, right up to the day of the wedding . . .

"Well, she's fine now. Fine." There was one more question; before he lost patience, she must ask it. "She told me the name of her doctor, but I forget."

"Dr. Hugh Sharon. Everyone goes to him. Went. Wonderful doctor, she's right, but don't try to ask him anything, since he had that stroke he doesn't practice, I don't even know where he moved."

Ask him anything . . . she realized it was for some presumable ailment of her own he expected her to seek out the wonderful doctor. She offered him her smile of formal gratitude, then she turned on a different sort of smile for Alan.

"Any success?"

"I'm getting started, anyhow. I still have to track down a Dr. Hugh Sharon, but he had a stroke."

"Track him down today?"

She shook her head vehemently. Definitely not today, she didn't even know where he was living, today had already offered all that could be expected or absorbed.

"Then we forget about business? Start enjoying ourselves?"

And of course he was right again. Lightheaded, vaguely triumphant, she wanted nothing so much as to enjoy herself, she felt serenely entitled to it. Enjoying oneself with Alan meant sitting back regally while he picked out the one creditable dish on the menu, laughing with easy delight at his stories, accepting the occasional rebuke of his scrutiny.

"Why do you wear your hair like that?"

"Now what's wrong?"

"Oh, it's fine. Lovely. But remember that bun you used to sort of toss on top of your head?"

"That sort-of-tossing procedure took me twenty minutes before a date and half an hour with curlers every evening."

"Worth every second," he said, and with his declaration, that girl who had walked along with her arms full of books, and her hair contrived and shining, and her greeting demanded of so many people between the library and Dedham Hall that sometimes she was late for her next class—that girl was back. Or, if not exactly back, she was recalled with affection, evoked as an example. Jane Bassett was not so distant from that girl. Just because someone went marketing in a baggy skirt did not mean her glamor must be permanently behind her.

And just because someone sat for most days in a playground didn't mean that on other days she couldn't have the kind of date that was the perquisite of anyone young, bright, pretty. In Stoneycrest, she thought suddenly, girls had dates like this all the time—it was easy to imagine them as you drove down some shaded street, saw the women standing in their circular driveways. As she and Alan walked out of the hotel together, a visitor looked over at them, smiled. Why not? The two of them coming down the steps were a natural part of the spring afternoon, like the sun filtering through the branches of that maple, the dog lying drowsy on the porch, the wild flowers making a carpet along the bottom of that stone wall. The spectacle of two attractive people in a tan convertible, in fact, so belonged to the fine day, was so in tune with it, that Alan's kiss, when it came, seemed an inevitable part of the scenery too, merging with it. Afterwards, she watched his face draw slowly away, relapse into contentment.

"Much better," he said.

"Better than what?"

"Racing in the Everett's yacht. Jib up, jib down."

She sighed. "Right now I ought to be out in the playground. Talking French."

"So the children won't understand what you say?"

"So our minds won't go to pot. Linda says it's important, we even have to think in French."

"Keep Linda happy—isn't she the one who'll babysit when you meet me next time?"

It put things in a new context—she moved to the other side of the car. "Alan, I couldn't do this again."

"You don't like it?"

"Of course I do. But—"

"Then what's the matter with next week?"

"Alan, it's out of the—"

"I know. You have to be on a business trip. Do research at a hotel desk. That's if you consider it in English. But do what Linda says—think in French. A date with Alan in New York . . . try it on for size in some Latin language."

That was Alan. If she had said they were studying African history, he would have found a way of exploiting that too. It was what you had to do in business: seize the angles, turn them to your advantage. Why had she thought such a process was crude—what went on was very much a game of wits, an intellectual exercise. All this plus—what had he said?—determination: you could see how Alan, once he had determined to go after something, would prove so shrewd and determined that the person at the other end might just figure there was no point in putting up resistance, in the long run Alan would get his way anyhow.

"Alan, today I had to come, I had a reason."

"I'll think of another reason for next week, leave it to me."

A pleasure to leave things to him—look how well they turned out. In her mind, it all fused happily: Alan's helpfulness, the disclosures about Doreen, the bright talk on the way home, even Alan's bland assumption that he would be seeing her soon again . . . all were part of a successful day, each part had been perfect. In fact, when Tony walked in that evening, she didn't even think about a gradual build-up, she burst with an excited voice and an enthusiastic face into her recital.

"I found out about Doreen. Only guess what, Doreen's not her name at all, it's really Doris."

"That so?" He put his brief case on the desk, next to last night's pile of unfinished homework.

"That's only the first of the little lies—"

"Jane, I had a meeting with Simon, and then three kids for tutoring; I'm starved."

"I just got in ten minutes ago, dinner might be a little late."

"Where were you till ten minutes ago?"

"Tony, I told you. I was finding out about Doreen." No: she had not told him; she had simply felt her fervor was so strong it must in some way be imparted to him. "Doris . . . her real name . . . that's only part of it. The other thing is, she caused the accident."

"What accident?"

"Remember, Tony, she was standing right here in this kitchen when she mentioned it. And it was her own carelessness, only maybe carelessness is not the word at all. Because she knew better. She wore sandals to go up a slippery mountain even though anyone could have told her, in fact, someone did tell her."

"Who told her?"

"The fellow at the desk." From the look on his face, still too fast. "She was looking for trouble, don't you see? The kind of trouble that would ensnare Martin. For all we know she made herself fall. She wanted to get hurt, so she could have him feeling thoroughly guilty, he'd have to marry her."

"What desk are you talking about?"

"If you're going to take that antagonistic tone, I'll drop the whole thing."

"Okay," he said reasonably. "Then let's eat."

"Tony, dear, the desk at the hotel in Vermont, which other one would I—"

"You called up there?" He opened the refrigerator and closed it.

"Heavens, people don't confide in you on the phone, you know that yourself. I went up there."

"All the way to Vermont?"

She ripped the cellophane bag off a head of lettuce. "Not so far—three hours each way. I left at eight-thirty sharp, I even had time to market before—"

"How'd you get there?"

"Tony, you're not even interested in the main point. I thought if we could track Doreen down, find out what she's really like."

"How did you get there?"

"With Alan. Alan Grant—you remember him."

"Can't say I do."

"From college. He was in the Eco department with me—now d'you remember?"

"He just conveniently happened to show up, eight-thirty this morning?"

"I ran into him yesterday, silly." She had to raise her voice, over the sound of water splashing on the lettuce. "He has some friends up here, he's up for a few days of—"

"Then you knew yesterday you were going—last night—and you didn't say anything."

"Tony, you keep concentrating on all the little things. . . ."

"Is that what I keep doing?"

She was conscious of his gaze, as she turned to lay plates on the table. "Don't think it was so easy. All that elaborate planning. I had to have Mrs. Bowers first, and then Linda took Betsy to the playground, and then, from three-thirty on, Sheila."

"Very hard day. I understand."

She made herself look up. "Tony, listen. I thought you'd be happy."

"I certainly am. Delighted. I come home and my wife tells me she's gone off to Vermont with Alan Grant."

"I thought if we could track down Doreen's lies."

"Tracking down lies. Yes. I'm always interested in that."

She could feel the incipient tears, and the only recourse, the only way to forestall that inadmissible weakness, was in a voice of detachment.

"Never mind, I won't even bother telling you the rest of it."

"I thought you did tell me all of it. She changed her name. She wore the wrong shoes. What more is there?"

What more, indeed? It had seemed so consequential, so fraught with meaning—with the force of a great revelation, the man's words had come to her across a pile of wicker baskets on a hotel counter this morning. But like all revelations, must it remain private, incomprehensible to anyone else? For a second she trembled, seeing the whole day through Tony's disenchanted eyes, feeling the import of its discoveries dwindle.

"She told us she couldn't have children because of the accident—remember her saying that? Well, maybe that's one of the lies too, it's how she made Martin feel even more guilty so he had to stay with her."

His eyes went over her coldly. "Jane, this is the most speculative kind of hypothesis, it's based on no evidence at all."

"We could get evidence. We could try to find out."

"What kind of excursion are you planning to make with Alan Grant in order to run this particular evidence down."

A sharp effort to control the tears again—then the requisite fury was summoned. "Okay. If you want to be so small-minded. Petty—just go right ahead. I was worried about my own husband. Thinking that for a whole week we hadn't once . . . we hadn't . . . I wanted to change things between us, that's what I wanted. But you wouldn't be interested in that, why should you? You enjoy doing things for Doreen. You can be as protective as you want. Satisfy all that masculine vanity."

"That's unnecessary."

"Doreen wouldn't talk like this, would she? Such a brave little thing, I mean, she's so sweet and helpless about everything, she makes you feel really masterful."

"Oh, shut up."

It was the worst fight they had ever had. She turned back to the sink, seeing her hands shake as she held them under the uselessly running water. It was the worst fight they had ever had, and yet, standing stiffly with her back to him, feeling with the certainty of three years of closeness the vulnerability of his look, she realized things could still be patched. Talking, of course, would do no good; at some time words only existed to trip you up; even an apology—his apology, that is, because she certainly had no reason to make one—even the most contrite statement would come out grudging, forced. There was only one remedy; it had worked before, pulling them back from disaster. And impelling as this fight was, the remedy generated its own momentum too, swept along despite anyone's stiff pride or sense of outrage. Darkness and warmth and enforced closeness—what made her think you could write them off? They worked after all, they superseded everything.

She ran her hands along her hips, conscious of the thrill of expectance. It would not, of course, happen quickly. They would sit in rigid silence while they ate, and then he would say, gruffly, Here, I'll take that, when she bent for the garbage, and his arm would accidentally brush against hers when she hung up the dish towel . . . the whole tremulous ritual unfolded before her. She was furious at him, naturally—how anyone could be so obtuse, intolerant, dumb—but in a way all that would be part of the excitement. That man standing in the next room cold and unrelenting—it would be like making love to a stranger. There would be elements of assault—a semirape, almost. Her own husband assaulting her—a fitting culmination to a day in which she had listened to Alan's compliments, accepted his favors, felt his lips on hers. It was true: through exposure to one man, the susceptibility was aroused, strengthened, for another man to take advantage of. Another man: Tony—she breathed deeply as she heard him moving inside.

The phone rang while she stood at the stove. She walked slowly, dreamily, against the stirring in her blood—he was hanging up the receiver when at last she went in. "That was Staunton Hospital." He still had his hand on the cord. "Or, rather, some nurse. Doreen burned herself. It's terribly painful."

Homework papers were on the desk. He must have worked on some in school—sweeping marks from his red pencil across some student's painstaking handwriting.

"She was lighting the oven. I guess she forgot the gas was on. The nurse said would I come. That is, Doreen asked if I would come. Half an hour till visiting hours are over." Though his voice plodded through the jerky sentences, his eyes were unmoving on her face. "I have to go. Don't I have to go?"

"Suit yourself."

"It's not in the least what suits me, you ought to understand."

"I have my own life to lead, did you ever think of that?" she suddenly said.

"Jane, what's the meaning of that remark?"

"Oh, go right ahead if you want to. Go off and comfort Doreen, what difference could it possibly make to me." After he left, she looked for a second around the kitchen; she wasn't hungry, no reason to make supper. Then she went inside to where Betsy slept, pulled the spread off the day bed. She would be sleeping here tonight, and she certainly didn't want to wait till Tony came home to start fussing with sheets and blankets.

10

He sat on the uncomfortable chair, which was what the hospital provided for visitors to Semi-private. "Of course I don't mind coming, Doreen, it's no trouble at all." However, for the past three days it had been nothing but trouble. To stand consulting with doctors, to listen to details about fever and dressings, to rush through whatever was going on at school so he could fit into the unadaptable visiting hours here . . . No. That was not the worst of it. The worst was realizing his own indispensability; solicitude, it seemed, was first welcomed, then counted on, then taken for granted. By now he was part of the routine, like temperature readings, fruit juice, pills. "You again," the fifth-floor nurse said with a not ungrateful smile from behind her charts, and "I guess I don't have to show you the way," the nurse's aide said as he hesitated in the middle of the hall, and even the woman in the next bed, who sometimes was concealed by the curtain on its curved rod and sometimes wasn't, even she had said as he walked in this evening, "Isn't it lovely, such a nice young man."

I am not a nice young man—should he go behind the curtain and explain? I happen to feel guilty about her husband's death, I have a lot to feel guilty about, that's why I'm here. Or should he ask Doreen to explain: Doreen, please make the fiction of my niceness absolutely clear to her.

"It's wonderful of you to keep coming. I bet you have a hundred other things to do, a million, and here you sit with poor little me, I can never thank you."

He put his books on the floor beside him; unjustified praise, it turned out, was as onerous as unfair blame. If your motives could not be openly labeled, at least there should be some recognizable categories, some acknowledged cut-off point which divided expiation from simple niceness, marked off responsibility owed from generosity freely given.

Doreen couldn't understand this, she could not be expected to, but what about Jane? Satisfies your masculine vanity. Makes you feel masterful. . . . Jane should know better. Or did she know better, and was it a willful misrepresentation? I have my own life to lead, did you ever think of that? Suddenly he felt a terrible fear—in some unfamiliar way, it reached out toward the future.

"—attention to what I'm saying."

"But I certainly am, Doreen. That second day. It hurt so much."

"Excruciating. I didn't want to tell you, I knew how awful you'd feel. And when they changed the bandages. Like I was just a package, they were peeling paper."

"I guess they do what they have to."

"Burns are the most painful things, everyone says."

A dissenting groan from behind the curtain—possibly Doreen's neighbor wanted whatever honor accrued from having what was most painful. The groan brought to mind the image he tried not to notice as he walked in: gray hair, gaunt cheeks, wrist supine to receive the liquid bubbling with ponderous slowness through the tube. He hated hospitals. When Betsy had to be left in one after birth and they went back to see her, he would stare ahead with stiff apprehension. One more hall, darling, I'll protect you, Jane would say.

"And so callous, these nurses. If they'd just show a little consideration."

"Doreen, they do their best."

"The way they run in and out, half the time they're not even listening. For all they care, you could die."

Another groan from the unseen roommate either corroborated or denied this.

"So mean, all of them. I wish I could go home."

Actually, he wished it too. Though Martin had had hospital insurance, there were the inevitable extras, and on the first night it had been taken for granted that the nice young man would pay. He paid again last night—presumably she would expect that he stop at the cashier's office on the way out tonight. "I just don't know what I'd do without you," she would say, her face piteous on the pillow. Was it eighty-four dollars he was out so far? Or should he count the food package which he had no choice but to bring after she told him in grim detail about what went under the name of supper last night, and which would bring the total to eighty-five fifty?

"You're getting better, Doreen, the doctor told me."

"It isn't the pain so much, I don't want you thinking that. But the time. I mean, the business was beginning to do so well. Three parties scheduled for next Sunday alone, and Mrs. Loomis wanted that special coconut for when her husband came back from his trip, and Mrs. Ayles. You'd never believe about that darling Mrs. Ayles. D'you know how she heard about me? Did I tell you? From Mrs. Kennicott, on Waverly Road. You know, the one with a swimming pool inside the house. Imagine. Someone with an inside swimming pool, and she talked about little me. All that depending on your pies. The way it makes you feel. And all that rushing, pies in, pies out, no wonder I forgot about the gas being on. A million other things I was thinking when I lit that match."

"I can understand that." He could understand without listening—she had said all this last night, she would say it again tomorrow night. And ordinarily he could bear it, he would be going home after visiting hours to his own wife. But there was nothing ordinary between him and Jane these days. When he came home three nights ago, she was sleeping in the day bed. There he had stood, tired, strained, discouraged, and his wife was in another room. He waited a second in that doorway which was not a doorway. She looked the way she did every night when she got into bed first: face burrowed into the pillow, hair spread in ingenuous disarray across her cheek, back arched in the childish position that could in an instant be foregone. But it was an alien bed she was in, and she was foregoing nothing; though she must have known he was there, though he stood silent a few feet from her, not a tremor marred that even breathing.

I have my own life to lead, did you ever think of that? "Not an easy life, married to a teacher, you have to think it over carefully"—his own words came back, over a span of more than three years. And it was on him, of course, that the need for carefulness had weighed as he sat next to her on a bench behind the library. "Tony, how can a girl think when she's being married a week from Tuesday?" "I have to tell you, Jane—" "Are you trying to get out of it? Is this your way of backing out?" "Darling, listen. Being a teacher is marvelous. In some ways it's the most marvelous profession there is. But it also happens to be the most underpaid. You have to consider that. A teacher's wife can get to feel very cramped." "I'll have you, won't I? Every single—" "Jane, I wouldn't be fair if I didn't remind you. Because the life you lead here at college. All those men who call every minute, and shower you with presents—don't think I don't know. That physics major with his million-dollar trust fund, and the fellow in the admissions office, and the one with all those connections —what's his name? Alan? Married to him—to any of them— you'd be sitting pretty. Any time you felt like a fur coat, or a trip to Europe. . . . All right, all right, I believe you. I just had to say it this once, I won't think about it again."

He was thinking about it now, with a resurgence of that fear that constricted him, shortened his breath.

"—want to hear what I'm saying."

"But I do, Doreen. I want to hear everything. Mrs. Kennicott. Mrs. Ayles."

"A few customers will go, I have to expect that. But I'll start right in again, I really will. Couple of days at home, and I'll be right back getting out the orders."

She didn't realize, though the doctor had given the prognosis plainly. Two weeks without her doing any work. Two weeks in an apartment she could not afford, needing treatment that would cost money, expecting help that who besides him would be around to offer. When another groan came from the folds of curtain, he thought he was the one to utter that dispirited sound. The groan gave way to talking—a nurse must have come in. The talk grew louder, more explicit.

Stiff-lipped, he launched into diversions—then he realized Doreen's attention had diminished. She was not looking at him, but she wasn't looking, either, at the foot of the bed, where a nurse with red hair was standing. Astounding red hair—Doreen turned her head sideways, as if unable to bear the sight of so much splendor under the prim white cap.

"Well, well, well. If it isn't little Mrs. Cobden. Back again."

A twitch at the blanket from Doreen, but her profile was stony on the pillow.

"How are we feeling this evening?"

Still no answer. Was it his presence making the difficulty? If he were not here, would Doreen go into the same details as her uninhibited neighbor about what did or did not afflict her half an hour after mealtime?

"These little accidents happen, don't they? Where is it this time?"

Another twitch, then silence. That sullen withdrawal lay unfamiliar on Doreen's even features—he had never seen her do anything about emotions except display them freely, luxuriate in them.

"The wrist again? Or someplace else? Tell me where."

Doreen lay quiet, a petulant child, while authority, in white uniform, stared down. The teacher in him went out to authority: when they act like that at school, we keep them after, send them to the office. Or were the punitive aspects inherent here too—who knew what comforts might be withheld if a red-headed nurse were irascible.

The nurse, however, was leaving—he waited till she was gone. "What was that all about?"

"I told you how mean they are. Just heartless. Now you can see for yourself."

He stared down; on her pale face, the little pout and

simpering cheerfulness were returning. "She seemed to know you."

"I had to come last year for some tests. Something with a gland, the doctor said. Well, glands, they have to find out, but was there any reason she had to keep sticking all those needles into me? Even when I begged her to stop for a second, I couldn't catch my breath? I mean, they can do things gently if they want."

It was too glib, it came with too bright an air of assurance; from the gusts of imprecise rumor that swept through hospitals, she had caught hold of one convenient word: glands. Doreen, which gland gave you trouble—suppose he put that forthright question. No. Doreen, which accident was that nurse referring to—that might be more to the point. And what if he called her Doris, how would the pouting expression alter then?

He gripped the rungs at the foot of the bed. Maybe that nurse had been trying to offer something—the same message Jane had offered as she stood making her shrill accusations in the kitchen three nights ago. Did they both have a point? Was there indeed some connection between a girl who would deliberately wear sandals to climb a slippery trail, and one who would have other little accidents later on? The idea formed, became clearer, vanished in an image in which Jane and Alan Grant were riding along some country road together, on a date she had tried to belittle, had brought out with conspicuous reluctance . . . a date she might not have mentioned at all unless she had to.

Suddenly he was grateful for Doreen's glibness—at least it cut discussion short. This way he could go easily, one walking out of a sick room with the murmured avowals of sympathy, the standard expressions of hope. The nice young man was tired, he had had his fill of equivocal suggestions and probing talk.

11

When the phone rang, she had everything ready to take to the playground: extra diapers, jar of apple sauce, blanket for the carriage in the unlikely event that it turned cold, French dictionary in the even more unlikely event that the talk would get elaborate. She let the phone ring twice; "You sure you remembered the dictionary?" Linda would say. Though ordinarily she bridled at Linda's authoritative handling, the emphasis on French, these days, had its advantages. "It is perhaps time to cut out the six o'clock feeding," you could say in the stilted forms and unsteady endings remembered from French 3-4, or even, "Her skin unfortunately breaks out after chopped spinach," but a discussion that started with "I feel a certain dissatisfaction with my life," was less probable. The censorship thus imposed was not unwelcome. It was only if you were feeling secure yourself, if things were all right between you and your husband, that you could endure from someone else the equivocal confessions and probing talk.

However, it was not Linda. "Janey?"

"Hello, Alan."

"You're in—I'm running in luck."

As she put down her bundles, she thought: it was not luck at all, careful research—someone else's research—would have informed him of the appropriate times to find the mother of a six-month-old baby at home. "I was just going down to meet Linda."

"It's about Linda I really called. To see how she is. Or rather, how she'll be next Tuesday."

"Next—"

"So you can leave the baby with her and meet me for lunch in New York."

"Alan, I told you. Out of the question."

"Why?"

"I don't know why, please don't ask me, it just is."

"That doctor lives on Eighty-fifth Street with his son and his daughter-in-law and two grandchildren named Ned and Stacey," his matter-of-fact voice told her, as if this had been the subject of their conversation all along.

"What doctor?"

"Didn't you say you wanted to locate a Dr. Hugh Sharon who used to be in Vermont but had a stroke?"

"Alan. I didn't want you to go to all that—"

"No bother. I just got someone to find out."

She gripped the receiver. How big a secretarial staff, how many long-distance calls, what network of knowledgeable contacts, till he just got someone to find out? "I can't let you do me any more favors."

"Even if they give me pleasure?"

"But I don't want to feel—"

"Indebted?" She had a picture of his face, coming closer to hers, wearing a look of triumph. "All in your imagination, that indebtedness. To make whatever you want to out of it."

There was a pause. What did Alan imply she wanted to make of it? What had he been led to expect she wanted? "While you're considering about next Tuesday—"

"Alan, I didn't say—"

"—till then, how about a date with the two of you? You and the schoolteacher." He listened for her response, heard none, went comfortably on. "There's a musical opening Saturday night. My cousin's married to the producer. I'll send you two tickets."

Outside, there was a small tangle of traffic; a truck delivering kitchen furniture had parked diagonally across the street.

"You're right to hesitate, might just be a lemon. But the party after, you'll like that, I think."

He was, of course, still exploiting opportunities—from a

phone thirty miles away, he could do it. He knew, he must know, how she would feel about such parties: the person sitting next to you on the couch turned out to be the playwright, and the girl who asked for a bobby pin while you both were combing your hair had done the choreography, and the man who said were you sure you didn't want another drink materialized, after fifteen minutes of witty talk, into the director that every columnist was writing about this season. This party would get into the columns too. . . .

He might have been watching her, observing her expression. "I couldn't go. Really."

"You used to be such a party girl, Janey. Remember that Sunday night I called, and ten minutes later there you were, with that bun on top of your head, and the black satin dress."

She giggled for a second. "I still have that dress. Been in a cellophane bag for three years."

"Take off that flower in front, makes the waist look too high. Otherwise it'll do fine."

She had never known anyone to make her feel so observed, analyzed, studied. "Alan, dear, Tony wouldn't want to come."

"You mean, you wouldn't want to bring him?"

She listened to the truck outside, but what she heard was the frosty note in Tony's voice: "Always interested in tracking down lies. . . ." "I mean, too many complications," she said.

"I'll save the tickets in case you change your mind."

He sounded entirely amiable, as if she had said yes to all his proposals. Or as if—the thought insinuated itself sharply— he knew that eventually she would say yes. "That Dr. Sharon —what do you want to find out from him?" his unemphatic voice continued then.

"Alan. No reason in the world for you to—"

"Because if you should decide to come to New York next Tuesday—I mean, if you should make that absolutely sensible decision—I don't want you to waste your time trudging up to East Eighty-fifth Street when I can find much better restaurants in the Forties."

His arguments made such sense, his voice was so reasonable and his claims to friendship so persuasive, as she stood in her living room waiting to go down to the playground. "Dr. Sharon took care of a girl in Vermont four years ago. Doris. Or maybe Doreen. She got hurt while she was mountain climbing, and she was laid up for a while, and when she got better she married a schoolteacher named Martin Cobden. And what I want to know is, did the fall leave her with any permanent injury? Did the doctor tell her she couldn't have children? Did he tell her and her husband?"

"Okay. Easy."

Of course: easy for him—just a matter of giving orders, spending money, dictating memos. As she leaned on a flimsy shelf of the room divider, it occurred to her that the facts thus procured might be wholly unserviceable for Tony. For her to have a date with Alan in order to get information was bad enough. But for Alan himself to be able to get that information offhandedly, with the expenditure of no more effort than the scribbled voucher, the folded check—that would conceivably cause more pain than even Doreen's machinations.

"I'll call you, Janey."

Too late to change her mind now. The process was already started by which Alan's connections and shrewdness were again doing her a favor.

12

"You're sure of it?" Angie said.

"Absolutely. Two hours in the Superintendent's office yesterday, Doreen wanted to make sure she got everything out of the retirement fund."

"Tony, you're too nice, I swear."

"I had all Martin's files, and no courses listed. Not a mention."

"What do you get for sitting like a zombie at those courses? I mean, how does the Board bribe us?"

"One fifty each—'for any course taken to enhance the professional worth of a teacher' is the official come-on. So that's three hundred dollars Martin passed up because he neglected to fill out some forms." He put his register into the middle drawer. "Doesn't sound like Martin."

"On the contrary. Sounds exactly like him. Elusive. Complicated."

"Then you don't think he just forgot? He was careless?"

Angie stood next to the window in the dress that would have been a difficult shade of green for anyone and was disastrous with her complexion. "I think what I always did. That the last thing Martin would do with a Tuesday or Thursday afternoon was listen to some idiot professor of education give a lecture about the theory of learning."

"You mean, all those months when he couldn't stay around . . . he had to run off for the three-seventeen? . . ."

She shrugged.

"Angie, if you had these doubts, why didn't you say something?"

"Like what? Accuse him? Tell him he was using false pretenses to get out of a four-o'clock meeting?" She tugged at
the zipper of her dress.

"But to keep those suspicions to yourself for a whole
year . . ."

"That's the business of being a spinster, Tony—didn't you
know? To work up suspicion of everyone. Have doubts about
the lives married people are leading. It comes natural, it's the
way we get our kicks."

Does she have doubts about my life? Does she sense the
elaborately casual manner with which Jane told me about her
date with her rich ex-boyfriend? Does she know that casualness is all there is between us, because we're not sleeping
together any more, we haven't slept together for weeks?
. . . . It was nonsense, of course, his private misery was his
own. Still, he moved across the room, out of reach of her
scrutiny. "We can find out definitely about the courses, I
guess. Check in New York."

Another shrug, under the bilious green—then she turned to
him. "How about that silly wife of his? Doreen. How's she
making out?"

"Doctors thought she'd be fine in two weeks but here it
is almost three, she still can hardly move the arm."

"Must be a hell of a lot of extra expense. Who's paying?"

I am, of course. Person who's responsible. Or didn't he have
to say it, was Angie making shrewd guesses, as usual? "Things
will get worse with Doreen," he evaded. "She can't handle
that little business for a while, and she still needs treatment,
and she's in no condition to move, poor thing."

"All this about poor Doreen—poor you we ought to think
about," Angie said sharply, and even while he disavowed her
sympathy, murmured that it wasn't needed, he thought: more
than I get these days from my own wife.

Then he realized Angie was offering not just sympathy but
a plan. A collection, in fact, to raise money. "We'll milk
the parents whose kids had Martin this year and last."

"Can we do that?"

"Why not? Collecting funds for teacher's widow—what could be more worthy. Jane'll help, won't she?"

"Oh, yes," he said quickly. "Yes."

"People around here, biggest favor you can do them is tap some of that extra cash." She tugged further at the unaccommodating dress. "You know that carnival they have every year at Junior High—biggest problem isn't doing the collecting, the dough pours in. Problem is what to do with it. . . . Tony, take off that skeptical look. School already has six motion picture projectors, two slide projectors, half a dozen tape recorders—what they're desperate for is causes. A widow without a cent—they'd jump at it."

For once she had misread him: he was not skeptical but weary. However, he listened as she went on. Two committees. Phone calls. Visits. . . . Then he frowned. "Why Steve Slocum on the committee?"

"Very persuasive fellow—who'd refuse him? Besides, Tony, the two of you—our prize exhibits."

The two of them: it was an added irritant—the same Board meeting that had voted him Head of the English Department had chosen Steve Slocum Director of Guidance. "I thought only friends of Martin's. Close associates."

"Steve was close enough to Doreen."

He knew his surprise must be visible on his face.

"If you're not close to someone, do you have them in your office a whole hour at your busiest time of day? Three o'clock —that's when Doreen saw Steve just a day before Martin died."

What was Angie hinting now? What new theories was that sardonic mind spinning?

"Tony, don't you believe me?"

"Of course, but—"

"More than an hour, now I think of it. I was due in Room 35, they said they'd mimeograph some tests, that's how I happened to see Doreen go into Steve's office. And those dimwits in the Business Department, nothing done when they promise, so that's how I know it was almost four-thirty when—Tony, you look terrible. Anything wrong?"

"Everything's fine." However, at three o'clock, despite the students waiting to see him, he went across the building and up to the third floor. If it were Steve coming to pry information out of a colleague, there would first be the circumspect preface, the disarming and irrelevant questions. How was Hester doing since that outburst in the gym? Was he still having trouble with the Evans boy? Did he know that Marilyn Hammer and Barbara French were the last to have been picked up at the Staunton Motel?

However, sitting opposite Steve in the small office, he knew the only way for him was to come right to the point: Martin's death presented some uncertainties, there were puzzling aspects to it, he wondered what Steve knew about the Cobdens that he hadn't so far disclosed.

"Disclosed to whom?" Steve regarded him affably.

"Anybody. Me."

"You going in for detective work on the side, Tony?"

"Martin was a close friend. I'm interested. Naturally."

"That close friendship—you're in a position to know more than I do."

"Martin was evasive. I was his friend but he didn't confide in me."

"I can assure you he never went in for heart-to-heart confidences in here either."

He looked around the room. There were curtains over the glass panel on the door—otherwise only the ubiquitous files, the stacks of memos, the view outside the window, of a muddy corner of the track field. "If you were seeing Doreen, I assume it was so she could talk about Martin."

"That's a dandy assumption but it just happens to be wrong." Steve tilted back in his chair. "Come to think of it, you've been seeing Doreen a bit yourself. Cute little thing like that, do men like us need a reason?"

She's not a cute little thing, she's a birdbrain. . . . If he said this, he would only expose his own motives. Was there any way to deprecate Steve's alleged susceptibility, and still maintain the fiction about the nature of his own attentions? Steve was watching him. "That's a public high school for you. Everything public—even a guidance counselor and his little flirtations. Still, I wonder how you knew about my seeing Doreen. Did she mention it?"

"Angie did, as a matter of fact."

"Trust Angie. Those old maids, they always know when someone is having a little extra fun, they can spot it a mile off."

He sat silent. A little extra fun with Doreen—it was a lie, of course. She was far too stupid, she could never appeal to someone so sophisticated, the last thing she could get started was a flirtation with Steve Slocum.

Suddenly he realized how many lies had been collected: Martin lying about his courses on Tuesday and Thursday, Doreen lying about the nurse in the hospital, Steve lying about his reasons for seeing Doreen, even his own lie about Rivers Street. . . . And what about the lying on Jane's part? *Just happened to run into Alan Grant while I was marketing.* Where else was she just happening to run into him these days? What else was going on, to give her that edgy tone, that withdrawn look, as she sat opposite him night after miserable night at dinner?

"That Doreen. Nothing seems to bother her." Aggressive, cheerful, Steve continued. "Most people around here are all wrapped up in their own neuroses. But Doreen—she doesn't know what a neurosis is."

Another lie; also, another device for testing him. *Did you know them when they lived on Rivers Street?* . . . the same appraising look in Steve's glance, the same derisive casualness in his tone.

"Don't you agree?"

"I guess so."

"All this mental anguish—up in Vermont they don't go in for it. Something about the crisp country air."

"Um-hmm."

"A pleasure to be with Doreen, I guess you found out. Relaxing. A shot in the arm."

He should never have come. He should have known Steve was too crafty to let him discover anything. Steve was deliberately baiting him with all this nonsense, and there was nothing he could say in contradiction or reply. When he stood up, Steve did also, walked with him to the door. At least a decent impersonality was restored: remarks could not have the same edge when students were walking by, footsteps were pounding, a girl was calling to another to Wait up, Wait right there at the locker or she'd kill her. Three boys passed, then three more, then one walking alone who gave a short greeting—they both watched as his slight figure walked the length of the hall.

Steve leaned against the door. "Interesting kid."

"Yes."

"You ever have him?"

"Bert Merimee, you mean? No, I never did."

"Martin had him last year." It was not asserted in the usual tone of jocular bellicosity—even Steve's face had softened. "Must have been a tricky year too. Boy was in very bad shape at the start of it."

"So I heard."

"Hostile. Troubled. Ready to quit school any second—I thought we could surely chalk him off. But little by little he straightened out."

"That's fine."

"Martin was part of what helped. Martin, the boy's innate sense, some other factors."

"I remember Martin mentioning him." I also remember the boy's mother standing in a doorway with her caustic remarks, her stony face. . . .

"Boys like that, there's always the heartbreaking uncertainty. With all the good intentions, you can lose them. Except then, of course, they're the lost ones."

He looked at the spot at the end of the hall where that

boyish figure had turned. He was through asking questions, they didn't help.

"Happen to notice the poem he wrote last month for the school magazine? About the ocean?"

"Yes."

"That business of a wave—an ambivalent wave not knowing till the last minute whether it would flatten out gently or smash with a roar . . . it's himself he's talking about. Bert Merimee. His own feelings of ambivalence."

"Very good poem, I agree." He felt wholly unsettled. The interview about Doreen had gone even worse than he had expected. Steve had not only presented a fraudulent picture of Doreen, he had also used all his craft to maneuver him, Tony, into tacitly agreeing with him, or at least not disagreeing. On the other hand, when Steve talked about the boy, he was wholly concerned, tender, even modest—if you were in touch with what went on along these corridors, you knew that among those "other factors" which had brought Bert around to stability, Steve Slocum played a very considerable part. The maliciously sly fellow who used his skill to bait his colleagues, the warmly sympathetic counselor who helped make the difference with mixed-up kids . . . could they combine in one person? Was there any way to reconcile them? Or would it turn out that the false Steve—whichever was the false one— must be counted as another of the lies, another of the troubling circumstances which one way or another had been set in motion by Martin's death?

13

Driving along Woodbine Street, Jane looked down at her beige silk dress, her high-heeled shoes. She looked nice, and she had worked at it. She looked like any of the women who drove along these shaded streets on their way to the golf club, the hairdresser, the beach. She happened to be on her way to their houses to collect money, and ordinarily she would have enjoyed it.

But what could be enjoyable when your husband treated you like a stranger? Even telling her about Angie's idea, he had spoken in his dispassionate tone, as if a collection for Doreen were of no more significance than one for a new music wing on the high school, new seats in the auditorium.

"Angie has it all worked out. Parents who had children in Martin's class."

"I see."

"Here's the list she gave me for you."

She glanced at the neat writing. "Anything special I ought to know about them?"

"Let's see. Hartley—a girl graduating this June. Goodenough —some lunkhead of a boy. Merimee—the father died two years ago, the kid's been in lots of trouble. A sensitive boy. Bert."

"Aren't they all sensitive?"

"This one's special." Tony's face had slipped into that look it always wore when he talked about children who moved him deeply; "They can go either way," he would say about them. What he meant, but was too diffident to add, was that it was very often the teacher who set the direction, made the difference in which way they went. It was the consciousness of this power, in fact, that sustained him through the days when study halls, absentee lists, wasted meetings seemed to constitute the bulk of his job. Tony, what would these kids do without you—she could feel the remark rise involuntarily to her lips. Then his expressionless face turned to her.

"Will you help us? Will you?"

There he was. Expecting the worst of her. Anticipating her refusal. "I suppose so," her bored voice said.

"I'll leave the car. Baby sitter gets paid for out of proceeds."

"Well, thanks." The build-up with Linda, however, had been very different. "What'll you wear?" Sitting in the playground, Linda had stared avidly. "Doesn't matter. Any old thing." "Jane, I don't know about you, but if I had an appointment at two-thirty with Mrs. Hartley." "Collecting money—you call that an appointment?" "You'll be there, won't you. In their house." "What's so special about—" "Grant Hartley—just happens to be an airlines president, is all. Jane, your beige silk, absolutely. And when she invites you for tea—" "Linda, I am not going for a—" "And get to the back of the house, don't forget." "Why the back?" "Don't you read the papers? This sensational sculpture garden, there was an article last Sunday. So your beige silk. You promise?"

She rubbed her hand now along the material. Despite some misplaced enthusiasm, Linda had sense; the dress was appropriate with the stretches of lawn, the banks where pink and white peony bushes were open, the set piece which on closer inspection resolved into a nurse and baby carriage. She drove slowly; two gardeners were sweeping bluestone on the driveway and a third appeared with a rake as she stopped in front of the steps.

A butler opened the door—yes, Mrs. Hartley expected her, would she mind waiting a minute. She waited in a hall studded with doors. Through that door would she go in her beige dress, her new hairdo, her fixed smile, ready to make appreciative comments about outdoor sculpture? Or this one, where she could see into the theatrical expanses of a gold-and-green living room?

"Mrs. Hartley said if you'd mind going in there. First door to the left—careful how you open it."

There was no way to open it except with care; a ladder was propped against it inside—on the top step a woman sat in dungarees.

"Sounds crazy, doesn't it, me painting the powder room myself. But we should learn to do things ourselves, I believe that firmly. If more of us did manual labor, in these days when everything is so— I haven't even introduced myself. I'm Melissa Hartley. You must be Mrs. Bassett."

She nodded.

"Watch out, something might drip. After all, only my first day."

Should she apologize for her unfortunate timing?

"So if anything gets on you . . . Now I can see you. My goodness. I mean, you're so dressed up," that accusing voice said from above.

Jane moved her dressed-up self closer to the door.

Mrs. Hartley flung an expressive arm, clothed in a new blue workshirt. "That color over there? Or this one? Help me decide."

She squinted into the light. From where she stood, no difference was discernible, but that flung-out arm was waiting. "I think that one."

"On the left . . . me too. More vibrant. And white woodwork, would you think, or the same color turquoise?"

"White."

"We really have the same tastes—you ever paint anything yourself?"

"No."

"You should try, really, you have no idea how satisfying. Oh, not a big room, at first, but something small like this. Unambitious."

She looked around. The window was recessed—did it open on the sculpture garden?

"This business of having every little thing done for us, so we lose touch with reality. Sometime why don't you try it? I mean, it's good for you. Therapeutic."

She nodded; she would try it, she knew she ought to say, she finally did get herself to say.

"Careful. I mean, if you keep standing there . . . Oh, you want your money, don't you?"

Not my money—she clamped her lips on the words.

"Foster? Foster?" The second call was unnecessary—from the alacrity with which he entered, the butler must have been waiting outside. He received in silence the information about which desk drawer contained a check, fetched it, returned: one hundred dollars for the fund for Doreen Cobden. She started to thank Mrs. Hartley, but on top of the ladder, activity had started again, a new streak of more-vibrant turquoise was making its satisfying way down a wall—she thanked Foster instead.

Outside, she looked at her list. Mrs. William Goodenough. A smaller house this time—no staff of gardeners in front, no sculpture in back, conceivably, even, no suggestions about the therapeutic benefits of manual labor, once she got inside. At the doorway, she paused. For what feats of industry had Linda singled out Mr. Goodenough? More important, what was to cement the affinity which, Linda had promised, was sure to spring up between her and Mrs. Goodenough: ". . . ought to hit it off, really, the two of you, just remember, Jane, that she—"

"Yes?" It was a maid this time.

"Mrs. Goodenough expects me. Jane Bassett."

"She's busy."

"I'm expected," she said firmly. "About the collection for Mrs. Cobden."

"Just a minute." She was waiting again. But a less quiet wait than last time. There was a radio playing past the half-open doors at her right, and above that the sound of women murmuring, and above that, presently, the clearly articulated sound of a woman's indignation. "They always come at the most inconvenient time, they have a talent for it, you can't sit down to a quiet game of bridge in the afternoon without them barging in to collect for this or that."

Barging in. Them. . . . Jane drew a breath. "I certainly thank you," she said to the maid who presently brought her a check. "It was a lovely visit, I enjoyed every minute, I'm so glad I wore my beige silk even though I practically never wear it, I save it for special occasions." Or didn't she say it? Did the blank expression on the face of the maid indicate that she had done nothing out of order?

Still in order, she got into the car. One more. Mrs. Bert Merimee. Mrs. Merimee had not been reached by phone, the note in Angie's handwriting explained. Should she, therefore, postpone this visit? It was not yet three o'clock—the last two stops had taken fifteen minutes altogether: Don't tell me you're back *already*, Linda would wail, if she drove up now to the parking lot beside the playground. The other two women had been charming on the phone, had said they would be delighted to see someone—how could this be worse?

In fact, as she reached the front terrace, she had the sudden assurance it was going to be better. A woman who could only be the lady of the house was on the lawn consulting with a gardener, but as soon as she saw someone drive up, she moved over politely, stood like any expectant hostess. Even a smile was conferred as Jane got out of the car, felt her heels dig into the resilient grass.

"Mrs. Merimee, I'm Jane Bassett. You don't know me, but you may know of my husband. Tony Bassett. He teaches English at the high school. We're having a collection for the widow of Martin Cobden—you probably noticed that he died some weeks ago. And I know the committee tried to get you by phone, they definitely wanted to call you first, but since I was right around the corner . . ." The attentive silence encouraged her—even a lawn mower had stopped, as though in deference to her words. The woman was elegant in blue linen, a bird perched in a nearby fountain, a dog slept under a beech tree, and in the opulence of this scene she felt her own sense of injury vanish. Linda was right: to come to a house like this, she should be wearing her best dress. This woman who looked so perfect herself would appreciate perfection in someone else. She waited while the dog roused itself, sidled off. Then her low voice went on. Terrible tragedy. Heavy expenses. No provision in school budget. The poor little widow.

Her low voice went on with such fervor, in fact, her presentation was so earnest, that her words had died away before she saw the expression on Mrs. Merimee's face. There was a moment of silence. Or not quite silence—behind a mass of shrubbery, she was conscious of the sound of a tennis ball, the shouts of voices. Something the matter there? Did that explain the sudden constraint? Then the woman reached into a bag on her arm, took out a small change purse, with deliberation separated two dollar bills from the rest of the money.

"What's this?"

"For the poor little widow." Mrs. Merimee was still rummaging through her purse. "No, wait. Here's some change. Sixty cents . . . let's see, seventy-five . . ." Then that elegant head turned sideways and found something of interest in the nearest flower bed.

It was too much. Anger choked her. Such ungenerosity. Such callous, petty ungenerosity.

No. You don't give a damn about the ungenerosity—face it. You care about the affront to you, Jane Bassett. You got all dolled up and you fell for Linda's nonsense: you had visions of yourself getting chummy with the Stoneycrest waterfront set. But you're just a teacher's wife and don't forget it. Lower class. What they consider lower class. If they consider you at all, that is. Sitting on top of their ladders, sending their maids in with their patronizing smirks, they don't know you're alive.

"I thank you very much." Her hands went ostentatiously behind her back.

"Don't you want it?" The money lay on the woman's outstretched palm; in the breeze, the two bills quivered.

"You might want to take off a couple of dimes. I mean, when you think it over."

"Is that Mrs. Cobden a friend of yours?" Mrs. Merimee unexpectedly asked.

"Someone doesn't have to be a friend if you show a little consideration toward them. Understand when they need help." The loftiness of her own tone carried her along, exalted her. And the woman did have the grace to look upset—under that beautifully arranged dark hair, a hint of some emotion flickered.

"Why doesn't she do the collecting herself?"

"Maybe she's sick. Weak." For a second she paused. This was Doreen she was talking about. Little Doris. Someone adept at staging the accidents, playing up the meretricious weakness. Then her own shoulders went back. What Doreen was or wasn't made no difference; it was Jane Bassett who had been insulted. "Maybe a woman might be in trouble, did you ever think of that?"

"The poor thing, it breaks my heart. . . . You going to take it or not?" Mrs. Merimee's hand opened again on the crumpled bills, the offending coins.

"On second thought, I won't take it, you've been simply charming and generous, I really do appreciate it, but I don't think I'll deprive you of your two dollars and seventy-five cents."

The woman's face was stony—had she gone too far? No: just what the situation called for. She had not done Doreen any good, and she certainly had not helped Angie's committee, and by tomorrow she might even be sorry, but right now, walking past the bushes blazing with flowers, she rejoiced in every haughty intonation and sarcastic tone. *I really told her off,* she thought. *I let her have it.*

14

"'By, Mr. Bassett."

". . . work too hard, Mr. Bassett."

"Good-by, Mr. Bassett, have a nice weekend."

They walked out fast; under their dutiful farewells was a true affection. It went both ways: theirs for him, his for them.

"So long, everyone." They were gone, of course. He looked around the empty classroom. Next year, if his present plan went through, he would be gone too. Someone else would be explaining to them about Hamlet, opening the door to poetry, discerning the one student in hundreds who would some day set the world on fire.

Someone else would do it, but not as well—briefly the irony came over him: if he weren't so good at teaching, he wouldn't now be able to do what he had no desire to do, which v s to quit.

"Of course I remember you," McHenry had said this morning on the phone. "Someone so talented, how could I forget?"

He gripped the phone. He had been calling from the public booth opposite the office. There was a phone in the faculty room, you could sit in comfort, but someone else could sit there too, figure out after a few poker-faced minutes that what Tony Bassett was talking about with such circumspection was a job for next year outside the school system.

"Too talented for what you're doing," McHenry's boisterous voice went on. "Too good for the schools—I knew it the moment I heard you at that meeting."

He put the phone close to his ear, though there was no chance of anyone hearing in the line of students outside.

There was always a line; as soon as they got to school they called home to say they forgot their lunch, banged up the car, needed their clarinet, couldn't keep the dentist appointment at three-fifteen.

"After all, that business of teaching—not saying anything against it. Someone has to do it. Fine profession for the women and misfits."

You couldn't agree and you couldn't disagree—he cleared his throat.

"Good man like you being wasted—what do they pay you?"

"Well, it's—"

"Never mind. Don't tell me." McHenry like to ask questions to which he then fended off an answer. "How's my daughter doing?" he had said in the meeting last fall. "She's getting—" "Never mind, don't say it, don't say it. I know—straight C student. Damn lucky she has a teacher as good as you, we used to be glad if she'd pull down a D."

"Wasted," he repeated into the phone. "You know what you're really worth? Fellow with your ability? Your appeal? . . . No, don't guess. Do not make a guess now. Plenty of time for us to talk about it."

"Okay."

"Just remember, Bassett, men like you have to get on in the world."

All right, then, it was settled—he would start getting on in the world. The world of linoleum promotion, marbled patterns, sales campaigns. He had never wanted any part of it, he had decided during his last year in college it was not going to be for him, but he knew now that teaching was out. "Bad enough you're teaching." The sacrifices involved were fine if your wife was sharing them with you, but Jane and he were sharing nothing these days. Not his hopes, not his thoughts, not his bed. His wife was not sharing his bed—over and over he had said it to himself this morning before he could bring himself to make the call. Why should she—all she felt for him was indifference. That pride she used to take in having her husband teach, that eagerness to hear about his work, that sense of sweet accommodation—all entirely gone. Maybe, indeed, they had never existed, it was only in his imagination that he had married a sympathetic girl.

"Well, yes," he said to McHenry. "Five o'clock Monday will be fine." Now he looked once more around the classroom. Plenty of changes ahead—some known ones and maybe some unknown ones too. For once he was glad he had promised Doreen to stop off there; distasteful as the visits were, they numbed feeling and foreclosed thinking.

Doreen was in her living room, lying in a sea of colored pillows. There was only a small bandage on her arm, which she held up wistfully for his inspection—the doctor had said by next week she could do everything. Wasn't that fine—she could start baking again.

"Certainly is, Doreen." He put his brief case down cautiously, next to an embroidered hassock.

Her languid gaze, however, failed to match his enthusiastic tone. "Next week . . . just seven days away." She stretched her feet, which were in open-toed sandals to match her dress. "I mean, all that shopping, and the oven going all day, and the phone calls—wears me out just to think about it."

He sighed; possibly she could limit the orders at first.

"Even so. You can't imagine how much pressure. The shopping alone. And you always forget to buy one little thing."

Maybe a list, he murmured.

"Gelatin, say—you have everything out on the table, seventeen different ingredients, and you realize you forgot gelatin. Know what that's like—to put down everything and walk three blocks to the store for just one little box of—"

"You were doing so well, Doreen."

Another languid nod. She plumped the pillow, which was the same color as her shoes and dress—no one had a better eye than she did for matching colors, she often said. "Maybe I could find something less taxing, I've been thinking it over."

"I see."

"Because it really wasn't so very profitable, was it?"

"Well, you—"

"When you figure the equipment I had to buy, and my own work. That was the thing—I was working practically steadily, sometimes till eight at night. When did I ever have a minute to myself?"

He gave a rueful sigh.

"So I was thinking I ought to look around for something a little easier, it's only fair, don't you agree?"

He walked back and forth. From the door he could see into the kitchen, where the new equipment was visible: baking pans, electric mixer, set of stainless steel measuring spoons, even the wall-type telephone which had cost four-seventy-five to install but would turn out to be a smart investment in the long run, she had explained, because suppose the phone rang just as she was pouring batter, and by the time she'd wipe her hands and run to the phone in the bedroom, some customer who had maybe wanted to order three pies would get impatient and hang up, didn't he agree? There was also an address book in a green and pink plastic cover to match the shelving—it was open at the C's. He went over and looked down: the top listing was Everett Cobden, Fresno, California. So that was where he lived, the fellow who couldn't be bothered coming East for a funeral. Not even his brother around to bury him—did nothing ever work out right for Martin?

When Tony went back to the living room, she had opened a sewing box and was fixing one of the pillows. "Listen, Doreen. What did Martin do on Tuesday and Thursday afternoons?"

"He went to New York. He was taking courses." Her pouting gaze bent over the torn seam.

"As a matter of fact, he was not taking courses. Not Ed. courses or any other kind."

"Who said so?"

"He never listed any in the Superintendent's office."

"Maybe he forgot."

"If you forget to list two courses you're out three hundred

dollars, so yesterday I called New York. He wasn't even registered. He had never registered."

For a second he felt the glance of someone distant, unknown, regarding him with hostility over the cluttered room. Doris, he thought. She looks like Doris. Jane had it exactly right.

"He told me he was taking courses, that's all I know about it."

"Did he ever talk about his work? The professors, maybe? The assignments?"

"He always said it was so hard at school, he didn't want to talk about any of it when he came home."

"Doreen, if you live with someone and they've made up a false destination, they've made it up for a whole year, they're sure to give themselves away somehow. Drop a hint."

"Martin's dead. What's the difference what he did on a few afternoons?"

"It wasn't a few. It was every Tuesday and Thursday for the whole school term. Thirty-five weeks, say, twice a week, when he must have—"

"If he said he was taking courses in New York, if that's what he told me, why should I think he was doing something different?" her resentful voice asked.

For a second he couldn't figure how to answer; the motion of her fingers, in and out, in and out, through the bright colors mesmerized him. "Fifty-five minutes on the train. A ride by subway. A chance meeting with someone he knew . . . must have been something he found to mention."

"I don't see why it matters."

All right, why did it? He stared at her small head, bent in sulky concentration over the sewing. "Because I want to get things straight, dammit. Can't you understand that?" He could see from her face that he must be shouting. "Sometimes people are simply interested in the truth. Because it's valuable in itself. It's important. It matters just by being the truth. Or wouldn't that mean anything to you?"

She turned her injured gaze on him. "I can get someone else, you could just have said so."

"Someone for what?"

"To help me go over these accounts."

"Doreen, for God's sake, what I'm talking about is completely—"

"I mean, I know how busy you are. And all the stuff they pile on you at school."

"If you'd just—"

"And I try, I really do. Before you came I worked for a whole hour on those figures. Adding them up. Subtracting."

"Crying out loud, Doreen, no one expects you to—"

"But the answers come out different every time. I mean, Martin always used to do it all. Just hand them over, he'd say. Bank books and store bills and everything."

Where in this room did Martin sit, he suddenly wondered. At the desk with its collection of ornamental ink stands? Here at the little table, squinting at the light from a pink lamp shade? Or did he take his papers to the window seat, did he try to find a space among the plants and the china cats?

"Maybe if they'd make instructions easier," she said. "But like with the medical insurance. Subtract ten percent of the top line, and add to forty percent of the—"

"You are completely misunderstanding what I was trying to say." He stood at the window. It must be close to five—the children were coming in from the playground, stepping over the low fences, cutting across the corners where the management was trying to grow grass.

"Or I could do housework," her thin voice said behind him.

He turned. "Now what?"

"Well, you're right, I agree, I really should be earning my own living. Not be so dependent."

"When did I say anything like—"

"You're right to be angry with me. Just sitting here all this time. Not making a penny."

"Jesus Christ."

"And I definitely have been thinking about it, don't think I haven't."

His head was throbbing; he pushed the window further open.

"I realize how unprepared I am, honestly, it bothers me too. So what I decided, some place right here in the apartments where they need someone to do simple cleaning. The women are always looking, you should hear them. Not scrubbing floors, I'd tell them right away nothing like that, but if two or three times a week I could just find—"

"Doreen, you are not going out to do housework, no one wants you to do housework, I never suggested that you do housework."

"Much better to stand at an ironing board than have you angry at me."

It was useless. He went over to the desk. "Okay, Doreen, let's start on those bank slips."

15

The start of another hot weekend, Jane thought. Hot, dour, uncompromising. She pulled the vacuum behind the lamp, and then, in the procedure they had adopted to avoid unnecessary contact with each other, made an arc around the desk where Tony was working. His head was motionless—he knew the rules too—but she noted the hair curling at the back of his neck. He needed a haircut; maybe after lunch she would tell him. And maybe after that, they could take Betsy to the beach—you didn't have to be on any particularly intimate terms with a husband to lie next to him at a beach.

You didn't have to expect anything to happen either, but a change of scene sometimes had curious results. The beach was crowded during most of Saturday but by five o'clock, when the people were gone and a pink haze hung trembling over the rocks, a family, feeling proprietory about its strip of sand, could stretch out at the water's edge. Lethargic, they could lie there with their bare limbs—it might just become the lethargy of tenderness.

Then she looked over his shoulder, saw what he was working on. "How much are we behind now?" The words came out before she had willed them.

"Pretty much."

"Exactly how much?"

"Must you know to the penny?"

"It's my concern too, isn't it? What slice of your salary Doreen is getting this month."

"My salary . . ." An odd look went for a second over his face—she had the feeling there was something he was not saying, something he might just say if she went tactfully after it. She had had a similar feeling when he got home yesterday evening—there were matters he might possibly discuss. But as he was fixing himself a drink, an emergency call had come from Linda: Linda's husband needed a sudden operation, Linda's baby was sick, no regular baby sitter could be trusted, would Jane come right down. Jane did, of course, go right down and stayed till midnight. So this was the first conversation between her and Tony in twenty-four hours, and look what a mess he had made of it.

Or was she the one? Was it her fault? Useless to speculate because his hostile gaze was already on her. "I suppose I ought to be grateful," she said. "We can always count on that collection Angie's running."

"What's wrong with it?"

"Such fun to go around to those people and beg for money."

"You're not begging for yourself," he said.

"They make you feel as if you are." All the grievances from yesterday suddenly welled up. "Being a teacher, a teacher's wife . . . in one of those houses, you count for nothing."

"Well, that's teaching. A fine profession for women and misfits."

She looked up at him sharply. It was not at all his type of remark; even allowing for the bitterness engendered by argument, it was out of character. Had all this fighting, then, so distorted him? I really don't mind working on this collection, she was ready to say.

"You trying to tell me you won't collect money? You won't do that either?"

Either: just what did he mean by that? What gave him the right to say it? "Fine collection that's going to be. One place, they offered me two dollars and seventy-five cents."

"Maybe you didn't ask nicely. . . . Okay, okay, I didn't mean it."

"Perfectly all right. No reason you shouldn't say what you think."

"Stop dramatizing everything. You know it's not in the least what I think."

She put away the vacuum; she had lost her taste for cleaning. "What does Doreen need all that money for anyhow?"

"We've gone over and over it, Jane. You know exactly how much Martin left. Didn't leave."

"She could cut down on expenses," she went on. "That apartment—you know what rents are there? A lot more than we—"

"Jane, can we drop it?"

"And the hospital, what'd she need a private room for?"

"It was semi-private."

"Why'd she burn herself. Any damn fool knows about ovens."

"She's not smart and efficient like you." He turned viciously back to his papers, and she thought, Was it just ten minutes ago I was planning the sweetly mediating effects of an hour at the beach. How did this fight flare up?—she couldn't remember. She stood beside him.

"Tony, it's so hot, I thought maybe this afternoon . . ."

He didn't answer.

"Late this afternoon, when it's not so crowded. You and I and Betsy—"

"We can't."

"You don't even know what I was going to say."

He was walking up and down, he wasn't looking at her. "Jane, Doreen has someone who'll buy her boat. That little motorboat—remember she talked about it? He'll pay a lot. Over eight hundred. But he won't take it unless she brings it to the Staunton dock early this evening. And she's afraid to manage it alone, she never has managed it—Jane, don't look like that, she really is inept, it's true. It might be the last thing we do for her."

"What do you mean by that?"

A closed expression had come over his face. "Will you come?" he said. "Couple of hours at the most. She wants to make us a picnic supper, she says we've done so much for her, now's her turn to—"

"I see. This outing is a favor to us."

"That's the way she wants to think about it."

He would accommodate Doreen's feelings, all right, make the little pretenses to salve her pride. "What about Betsy?"

"We'll get a sitter."

"Seventy-five cents an hour so I can have the favor of eating tuna-fish sandwiches in a boat with Doreen."

"Get Sheila, she charges only fifty cents. She's dying to sit for us, she always says she'll do it for nothing."

Sheila's eager face rose before her. Any time, Mrs. Bassett, just call me. The translation, of course, was: your wonderful husband, Mrs. Bassett, just let me do things for him. Usually it delighted her, this notion that adolescents so idolized Tony they were willing to cut prices to sit with his child, but nothing could delight her now.

"For once we're going to get out on a Saturday night, and you want me to spend the time on Doreen's boat."

"Jane, I know how you feel. But I have to do it. Even if it doesn't make sense—especially if it doesn't make sense—I have to do it. I thought you'd come with me. I even told her you'd come."

"Without asking me?"

"I'm asking you now," he said doggedly. He looked tense, and there was an odd quality about this stubborn request. Again she had the sense of his withholding something—of revelations that would be forthcoming if she would tactfully smooth the way. But she had been tactful; she had, she had. She was the one to translate into practical suggestion all the quivers of stifled affection. Indeed, what had she been doing for the past ten minutes except show the requisite humbleness, offer the mollifying advances, make the first overtures? He must know she was trying to make peace; if he had any feelings for her, he must know it. But not on Doreen's terms. Not under Doreen's auspices—couldn't he understand?

"Tony, tell her we're busy tonight. Take her in the boat tomorrow."

"The man who's buying it insists. He wants it tonight, and he wants to make sure it's in good working order."

"You're not the only one around who can handle a tiller."

"I'm the one she asked. The one who—"

"Oh, I know, I know. You're responsible for her husband's death, you have to do everything."

"Jane, listen. Maybe I won't be—"

"Besides, you just love doing things for her, it makes you feel so good. So protective."

"You keep saying that. Even though it's not true, you keep saying it. Maybe it's what you really want to think."

"The dear helpless little Doreen, she might not be so dear and helpless at all, but I can't expect you to consider that."

"Jane, the truth of the matter is—"

"Oh, spare me the truth about Doreen, I've been hearing nothing else for six weeks. Go out with her in the boat if you want, have a nice picnic supper, look at all those beautiful views of the Sound, just don't involve me in any of it, is all I ask. I mean, don't tell me another thing about Doreen because I can't bear it, I'm fed up with it, I don't want to . . . Tony? Tony!"

He was gone, the room was empty. She ran to the door, which still resounded from being banged. When she put her head out, she could hear footsteps—he was still on the first-floor landing. He would have to go slowly; the Bennetts left their carriage down there, and skates and bicycles from the Marsh boys were all over the place. In her mind he was walking slowly—she could still call to him, he would hear.

No. She would not call. Let him go and take Doreen out on a motorboat ride, since that was what he obviously wanted to do. Let him sit with her in that little seat, and show her how to work the mysterious contraption called a motor, and explain that it wasn't so difficult, nothing to be afraid of at all . . . let him put up with all her coy helplessness and at the same time eat the picnic supper she had prepared, tell her how simply wonderful she was to have fixed anything so delicious. Let Tony do all that, and his wife would make her own plans. Why not? It was only fair. No reason she should sit home alone while he was out in the sunset with Doreen.

However, as she sat at the phone, waited for it to answer, she thought: Is it true what Tony said? Do I know in my heart he doesn't like doing all this for Doreen, and am I just pretending to think he likes it? Am I pretending so I can have an excuse for doing what I want? . . . But by the time the doubts had formulated, the voice at the other end answered, and that familiar excitement was underway in her blood.

"Alan, this is Jane."

"Well, of course, who else would have me at the edge of my chair in a fever of anticipation."

"Do you still have that ticket for tonight?" Ticket . . . one ticket; all she had to say.

"Janey, love, it's damp. Soggy. For days I've been clutching it in my hand."

She had to laugh. No one was as good as Alan at fashioning the most genuine compliments out of the most unreliable facts.

"What time do you want me to come in?"

"As soon as you can change your shoes and shake out the black satin evening dress and get that bun fixed on top of your head."

"Evening dress . . ."

"If it's not in shape, Janey, don't worry; without it you'll still be the second-best-looking—"

"It's in fine shape." Take off the flower at the waist—was that what he had said?

"Then I can escort the best-looking girl, just what I like. That doctor told her she'd be fine after a year," he went on following a pause, but an infinitesimal one.

"Alan, what are you—"

"Dr. Hugh Sharon, from Harrod, Vermont. Didn't you want to know what he told that girl? Doreen."

"You didn't really—"

"You wouldn't want to go up to Eighty-fifth Street wearing a black satin evening dress."

"Alan, another favor."

"Do you want to hear or don't you?"

She shifted from one leg to the other. They had decided to put the telephone on a shelf of the divider in order to save buying another table; it was not till later that they realized this arrangement meant no chair in front of the telephone. Usually it was all right: for the calls telling Linda you'd be late, she should go to the playground without you, standing was fine. But there were times—a very few times—when you wished you had the extra composure and placidity that only a sitting position was able to confer.

"Of course I want to hear."

"Fine after a year—what the doctor said. This Doreen what's-her-name? She could do whatever she pleased, take any kind of exercise, have as many children as she liked."

"You sure?"

"What?"

"Nothing—go on." Of course Alan would be sure. He would be reading from a paper someone else had written. He could count on the accuracy of any research he ordered.

"But she should take things easy for a year because of some fall."

"She slipped on a mountain," she interjected and realized it was unnecessary. None of this had any impact on Alan; he would not see more human import in this than in the appraisal of a projected merger. In his mind there was no picture of a girl in sandals failing to get a footing on slippery rocks.

"Let's see . . . something else you asked." What new heading was he consulting, in those notes already filed in triplicate? "Yes. The husband," his crisp voice went on, and Martin was automatically dehumanized, the cynical glance and intelligent look reduced to a malleable statistic. "Dr. Sharon never did get to see the husband. They had an appointment for a consultation, but two days before it the doctor had a stroke, he was hospitalized for seven months."

She leaned her elbow on the flimsy shelf. "I couldn't have children because of the accident." . . . That was what Doreen had told her and Tony. Was it also the convenient lie she had contrived for her own husband? Was this her system for both increasing her husband's guilt and turning it to her own lazy advantage?

"Janey, everything all right?"

"Fine."

"I wouldn't have told you if I thought—"

"It's nothing, Alan." Or, if nothing, it was still hypothetical—Tony would be the first to point that out. Speculative. He would not be swayed by the kind of speculative hypothesis that cast doubt on the probity of Doreen. He felt responsible for her, and by now the responsibility satisfied a very real need of his own—he had made that clear.

Besides, she had already tried to set him straight about Doreen. The next installment—to which he might not listen any more than to the others—would be just as good tomorrow, the next day. Tonight she was meeting Alan. It was settled. And why not? A man who was so determined to please her that he would pick up her casual remarks, store them in memory, assign them to an elite staff for high-powered handling. Yes, she told him, the six-twenty-five was fine. Yes, the lower level information booth, she knew exactly.

As she hung up, she realized the extent of Alan's determination. It had already beguiled her into going to New York at a time when she had said she definitely would not go. There would be an expensive dinner, a publicized opening, a party— and what else? On what other plans for the evening was Alan's determined mind working? To what other proposals of his would she first offer a firm demurral, and then lend interested attention, and finally, perhaps, give a tremulous assent? She had a sudden inkling of how much the evening might mean, what changes might be in store. Did she want these changes? Was she prepared for them?

She went into the bedroom. Betsy was deep in her morning nap, the crinkle of plastic at the back of the closet could not disturb her. Dust, accumulated from many months, clung to the bag cover, but none on the sweeping skirt of the dress, the low neckline, the straps designed to set off bare shoulders. The skirt was too long—when last she wore it, she'd had the off-hand indolence of the assured college senior: you didn't have to get things perfect. She would settle for nothing less than perfection tonight; as she held up the dress, a great delight filled her. To spend time getting to look your best, to have a reason for looking your best—every girl was entitled to these joys. The busy day stretched ahead; she went to the phone and called Sheila.

16

"A redheaded nurse? . . . You really think with my busy schedule, I can help you find a redheaded nurse?" the woman at the desk said.

I have a busy day too, Tony did not say. I might have one of the busiest days of my life, and the last place I want to be is in a hospital. ". . . No, sorry, I don't know her name."

"Miss Arning? Miss Latimore? Mrs. Paine?" She pronounced them slowly, as though that must refresh his recollection.

He had nothing to recollect—how could he convince her? The name must have been pinned to a uniform as the nurse stood with her caustic expression, her striking hair, at the foot of Doreen's bed, but of course he hadn't looked. He hadn't listened either, or at least not with attention. When she had said, "Well, well, another little accident," he had been too wrapped up in the rigidity of his own preconceived ideas; he didn't realize that was the time to follow her into the hall and ask for an explanation.

He stood in the hall now, getting no place. "You don't know her name and you don't know where she works?"

"Three weeks ago she was stationed up here." He lowered his eyes when the elevator stopped: it might be one of the cadaverous-looking patients on a stretcher. But only a man carrying flowers came breezily through the door.

"Three weeks . . you know where she might be by now? In X-ray. Or over in the new wing for therapy. Or in the operating room. You look in the operating room?"

"No."

"They wouldn't let you in anyhow," she observed with satisfaction—did everyone get pleasure in making you look a fool? "Day shift or night shift?"

"I really don't—"

"Say it's day shift. Day shift on this wing. You know what kind of needle's-eye hunt it is?"

He had no choice; he had to play into her hands. "What kind?"

"Red head . . . now let's see. At last count we had six nurses with blond hair, eighteen with brown, a honey with black. But that was two days ago, by today we have eight nurses with brown hair . . ."

It was useless. He had made two other attempts already— if they didn't laugh at him, they got angry. This was a hospital, overworked, understaffed—no place for so trifling a mission as pursuit of a redheaded nurse. He walked around the hall, circled the cart bringing juice for mid-morning snacks, decided at the last minute against walking down the stairs, and saw her at the circular desk outside the elevator.

"You probably don't remember me."

It took her only a few seconds—then that fiery hair nodded under the prim white cap. "You're Mrs. Cobden's young man."

He watched her pencil draw zeros in the tiny boxes of a chart. Did it mean someone was getting better? Or was progress nil, could they turn the bed over to a patient more amenable to treatment? "Actually, I'm not her young man."

"Well, she'll see to it that you are, that type can always manage, if not by next week then the week after that. . . ."

"I know you're busy. If we could go someplace for a minute to talk."

"What's the matter with right here?"

Three lights were flashing above doors in the corridor, and a nurse's aide holding a clipboard waited for instructions, but obviously he had as much of her attention as would ever be available—dispirited, earnest, he leaned across the counter. She was quite wrong, he could understand the reasons for her mistake, but the fact was, his wife . . . he and his wife . . . some little discrepancies . . . On and on the argument went, and when he had finished, her pencil still was threading through the small cages, there was no way to tell whether he had made an impression.

"Because my wife and I have reason to think . . . that is, you mentioned that Mrs. Cobden had been here before. In the hospital. And we'd be very grateful." Again that presumptuous "we." How would Jane feel about being alongside him in spirit, giving tacit support as he followed these unpromising leads?

The pencil jabbed to a standstill. "She was here because she cut her wrist," the nurse said with sudden determination.

"I see." Something with glands, Doreen had said. Hear that, Jane? Doreen said glands but that's another lie, it wasn't glands at all.

"She was slicing bread and the knife slipped." For a second the nurse looked up, he had a glimpse of the gaze that had made Doreen retreat into unaccustomed silence. "Only it didn't slip down on the bread board, it slipped up and cut her wrist."

He watched that pencil, starting maneuvers again.

"The knife slipped—that's what the records show. You believe the records, don't you?"

"What do you think?"

"Nurses aren't supposed to think, we're here to follow orders. Someone else wants to ask how come so many accidents to one person, that's their business."

The lights still were flashing but there was now another nurse at the desk, she wasn't running to answer them either. "You mean there were other accidents before she cut her wrist?"

"Maybe yes, maybe no. I just tell you what I saw. First a cut, then a burn. A burn on her poor little hand. How did that one happen?"

"She was lighting the oven. She forgot the gas was on." How could you give an answer and still not seem to be offering a defense?

"Well, maybe. Maybe a woman can really forget how to

light an oven. But men like you, I can see, you'll go right on believing what she wants you to believe, you'll fall for it."

Her voice had continued so unemphatic it took him a second to realize he was being admonished again. All her distrust of him was back; like the malignant disease that might be behind any door along that hall, it could be allayed, even arrested, but after a while it would return, strong as ever. Men like him, she could always tell.

He could attempt to bring her around to his favor once more. While the aide resignedly moved her clipboard and the patients waited, unresigned, behind those futile lights, he could point out her error, explain how he—he and his wife, that is —really felt about Doreen. And after that he could go down to another desk, spend a couple of hours convincing someone of the necessity of Mr. Bassett seeing the complete file on Doreen Cobden. And then what? How much more corroboration did he need? How many more examples of the injuries that began in the ambiguous mishaps and ended up, for Doreen, with the convenient results? Besides, he hated hospitals, even with Jane next to him they were a torment. Jane wasn't next to him now, but soon she would be, soon she would be.

There was just one more stop; in the drugstore around the corner, he filled his pocket with change, closed the door of the phone booth. Dials whirred more quickly than he was prepared for; not even eight o'clock in California—I'll be waking them, he thought. But though Martin's brother, in a voice not at all like Martin's, said Yes, they had been sleeping, he also said he was glad to talk to a colleague of Martin's.

"More than just a colleague. Friend, really." It took on reality as he spoke. "Martin knew things—he had this amazing insight." How had Angie put it? "His being at the school raised the level."

"Bassett . . . I think he mentioned the name." Even if they weren't true, the words gave pleasure; brother Everett couldn't be all bad.

"We had rooms right next to each other. If my class made

a racket, Martin could hear. That first year, he'd tell me how to get them in hand."

He paused; no answer from Everett—had this efficient connection broken down after all? Then he realized the man was weeping; from a still-darkened bedroom in Fresno, California, came the faint sound of a brother's grief.

He looked out through the steamy pane—easy to allow some emotion to rise in him too. "I'd have liked to meet you. I'm sorry you couldn't come to the funeral," he said.

"I would have come, I told her."

Her: he can't like Doreen very much if from three thousand miles away he calls her "her." Then a more important thought struck him. "What do you mean, you would have come?"

"My only brother . . . I badly wanted to come. Saturday would have been fine for me and my wife too. But to leave our jobs on a Wednesday . . ."

See, Jane, how easy it is to catch her in lies. You don't even have to ask the questions, go through the tricky catechism. The lies are there, waiting to be snared. Or did you know it all along? "She said you weren't coming anyhow, that's why she changed the funeral to—"

"Doris said that?"

"Who's Doris?" Then, of course, he remembered—something else Jane had been trying to tell him.

"Oh, she makes you call her Doreen." With that venture into sarcasm, the man started to sound like Martin after all—he might have the same cynical look around intelligent eyes, as he sat on the edge of his bed in his pajamas. "Doreen—she tried it on us, when we came to New York to meet her. 'I don't care what Martin wrote you, from now on my name's Doreen. People's names can be anything they want.'" He could imitate too; he had seen her only a few days, but he had caught exactly that mixture of obstinacy and simpering coyness. "It didn't go over so big with us. Doris. Little Doris."

The disembodied figure at the other side of a continent stopped speaking, but the disdain he had raised came over the wires, hovered in the stale air. "You're sure she understood that you would come on Saturday?"

"Look, Mr. Bassett. I never liked Doris, I told Martin right away, but she's no fool. If you tell her you can't get there by Wednesday but you can make it by Saturday, she understands perfectly, she bases her plans on that."

"Why do you think she didn't want you to come?"

"Maybe she knew we didn't like her, that's one reason. Or maybe she knew that we knew Martin didn't like her, that would be a better one." At last he sounded tired, a man who had been awakened out of sleep.

Martin's brother was not the only one who had not shown up at the funeral, Tony thought suddenly. Her father was dead, her mother in a rest home, Doreen had said, but wasn't there anyone from that small town in Vermont who could make it down when a local girl lost her husband? Jane had driven up there and back in a day—not such a long ride. Not such a long ride unless, of course, you were not invited, a woman knew her best chance of maintaining lies was to have no one around to contradict them.

Absolutely right, Janey, you saw it ahead of anyone. Maybe he would not even have to say it. When he walked in, she would take one look and understand without his saying a word. She had been difficult lately, and she had flown on the most trivial pretexts into spiteful rage, and every time he made a peaceful overture she had somehow managed to ignore it, but when her husband came home this morning, she would know exactly what he had in mind. He said good-by to Martin's brother and walked fast through the crowds doing their Saturday shopping. Two seconds: all it would take her. She would find that blue-and-red rattle that could keep Betsy endlessly content—deftly, she would tie it across the crib. Here, baby, play with this, her crooning voice would murmur. I know you want me to pick you up, but your father and I are going to bed together, high time we went to bed together, please, baby, quiet for a little while. He could see Jane's face as she leaned over the crib, her fair hair falling across her cheek, her face suffused with the expectant look that only he could recognize.

But it was Sheila's face that greeted him. "Oh, Mr. Bassett, you scared me, I didn't expect—"

"Where's Mrs. Bassett?"

"She went to have her hair done."

"When will she be back?"

"Couldn't be for at least an hour more, could it? That is, forty minutes under the dryer, and with the manicure . . . everything had to be perfect for tonight, she said."

Stop hating this girl. Stop seeing all the defects in her round, adolescent face. None of it is her fault, she has nothing to do with it.

But some of the displeasure must have shone through. "She doesn't even need all that fussing, she's so pretty, Mr. Bassett, she's the prettiest one in this whole apartment, just about." Compulsive, zealous, Sheila blundered on. Then she raised her eyes hopefully, like any student who had spoken up in class and was now entitled to official approbation.

"Well, fine, Sheila. Fine." He pulled at a leaf on the ivy. Jane never had her hair done. This nutty town, a beauty parlor to every three women, can't they take out their own rollers, she would say. It signified nothing: no reason, on a Saturday morning when she was feeling injured, angry at her husband, a girl shouldn't want someone else to take out the rollers for a change. Then he went inside, past the set of *Dickens*, the dangling telephone cord. Betsy was awake, sucking on her fingers, but though her face wore the placidity that always seemed to him most beautiful, he couldn't keep his gaze on her.

"Beautiful, isn't it?" Sheila didn't refer to the baby either.

"Yes."

"At first I liked it with the flower at the waist, I said she ought to keep it, but now it's off I see she was right. Looks much better without the flower, don't you think?"

Swaying from its tissue-wrapped hanger, the dress stretched halfway down the closet door. For three years Jane hadn't taken it out of the bag. Sometimes she would push the bag

aside when she cleaned, he could hear the faint crackle of
plastic, but there was not even a wistful look, a longing sigh,
to give a husband any warning. Or had the wistfulness been
there all the time? Was it just another sign of his obtuseness
that he had not noticed?

"The length, too, she's right about it being too long."

"You think so?"

"Be a lot of trouble, that rolled-up hem, she'll have to pin
every inch, just about. She said she didn't mind."

Indeed, she had started already; some of the pins were on
the floor—a folded packet, and around it the stray pins, gleam-
ing on the floor boards. Sometimes they put Betsy on the floor
to crawl—how dare she leave pins there, he thought furiously.
Then he realized how close he was to an irrational outburst—
he went back to the other room.

"And I don't mind staying late, like Mrs. Bassett asked me."

"Is that what she asked you?" A stranger in his own living
room, he stood awkward in the doorway. I have better things
to do with a Saturday night than go out in a boat with Doreen.
I have better things to do with a Saturday night than go out.
. . . All right, he got the point—couldn't she stop saying it?

"Might be very late, she said, you just can't tell." Still volu-
ble, eager to please, Sheila looked up at him. "Isn't that right?"

"Right," he said. "You just can't tell."

"And please don't worry about me because I have all this
work—see, two chapters in Chemistry, and I brought the poetry
anthology."

Dimly he saw the familiar landmark: the scuffed green binding, the faded letters. Again he knew some commendation
was called for: a girl choosing poetry for Saturday reading.
He made a great effort. "Good for you, Sheila."

"I just never realized poetry could be so exciting. When I
think I almost didn't take English with you, I was going to
have another teacher. But Mr. Slocum was the one."

"What one?" Another second and he could go. He had to
get out of here, he must not be around when Jane came back
with her perfect hairdo, her manicure.

"He made me change my whole program so I could have you."

Her words buzzed annoyingly at consciousness—you brushed them aside and they came insistently back. "Mr. Slocum did what?"

"It was when I was having that trouble last year. Remember, flunking French, and with History? And Mr. Slocum was wonderful, he saved my life, just about. He said, 'There's one superlative teacher in this school, he's the only one who has the intelligence to do a first-rate job, and if you know what's good for you you'll see to it that you get him.'"

He looked again at that open face. In class, her work was accurate, plodding, derivative; she had a well-trained memory and no imagination at all; however much she wanted to please a favorite teacher, she would be incapable of making up this kind of story.

He gave the fatuous nod of a man deprecating a compliment —then Betsy gave a little cry, and he thought for an instant of going in to her. But of course Sheila was here to do that. Sheila was here for the day and until late tonight—was this the way it felt to be dispossessed? "Well, good-by, Sheila, take care of everything."

"Oh, I will, Mr. Bassett, I definitely will."

17

"Like it, Sheila?"

"I do, Mrs. Bassett, I definitely do."

"I took big stitches in the hem. Can't tell, can you?"

"Mrs. Bassett, you're beautiful. That dress. So slinky and—I don't know how to say it."

"Sophisticated?"

"That's right. And your hair, the way they fixed it, all that wonderful business on top."

"A little piece isn't mine. They had it at the hairdresser, just the right color. Don't tell, Sheila."

"Oh, I won't. Only I never realized, seeing you around every day on the playground."

No one realized—that was the trouble. This was Jane Bassett too, this girl in sophisticated black satin, silver shoes, a bun of contrived and cunningly blended hair.

"Shelia, you remember about the ten o'clock feeding—nothing unless she wakes up and cries."

"She's so good, she never cries." To prove her devotion to Mr. Bassett, Sheila would even go in for a minor inaccuracy about his child.

"You're sure you won't be tired?"

"I might just take a nap. And I have all my books." However, at mention of books, some of that eagerness was dimmed. The girl pointed to the familiar green binding—poetry? literature? grammar?—and a hesitant expression crossed her transparent face. Why isn't my wonderful Mr. Bassett part of this picture of elegant glamor—was that the question it took all her tact to refrain from asking? What kind of arrangement is it that has a wife going out alone in her sophisticated evening dress?

Jane stood stiff in the doorway. Almost eight hours had gone by since Tony had walked out in his wholly unjustified rage. She had no idea where he was, what he had been doing. Had he even stopped off at home sometime during the day? There was no way to put the question without starting more confusion in Sheila's troubled mind. Better this way. Tony was out—of his own choice, he was out—and now she was going out, and whichever of them came home first could give to this little baby sitter any explanation that was needed. That was as far ahead as she would look.

"Fine, Sheila, you take a nap the second you get tired."

She swung her beaded bag. On the way down to the taxi, no one saw her, but if they did she wouldn't mind. Jane Bassett, in black satin, off to a date in the city. All over Stoneycrest, girls were going out like this—casting last-minute looks at mirrors, gingerly holding up long skirts, wearing the small private smiles of elation. Yes, dear Alumni Representative, since you asked me, I can say I'm having a very interesting life, just the kind of life for one who was a VIP in college. First an expensive restaurant, and then theater, and then a party for the cast, and after that . . . well, it's all part of the interesting life, too. For a pretty girl, certainly. She can't just spend her days with washing machines and babies. She has to get out once in a while, accept what happens.

She stepped into the warm evening, and she realized sharply what could happen. Men like Alan didn't underwrite extravagant favors just so they could sit talking about old times with an amiable classmate. It was true she had called him this morning, but if she hadn't, he would have found some way to make himself available—all the groundwork had been laid. I'm a very determined man—the extent of Alan's determination came over her, she realized how little she was prepared to protest against it. She was not going to protest—suddenly she understood that.

And while she was giving in, submitting to what Alan proposed, Tony would be—eating tuna-fish sandwiches in Doreen's boat. She sighed, sitting back in the taxi. Tuna fish: she had said it in spite, but it was just as far as Doreen's imagination would extend. With deviled eggs, and little cookies with colored sparkles on top, and lemonade in a plastic thermos. Oh, it's fine, Doreen, Tony would say bravely, but his face would look pained, under those disheveled eyebrows his eyes would narrow in distress.

Only why was she seeing Tony's face? It was Alan's she ought to hold before her. Alan's face wearing that sweetly triumphant smile as he ordered wine, nodded to his cousin's husband in the row in front, introduced his pretty friend to the producer. Tony, go away, I'm not supposed to be seeing you, that's not in the least why I got all dressed up like this. Tony, you can look as miserable as you want, it's your own fault, just stop bothering me.

He didn't stop. His face was there: the lowered eyelids, the tight mouth—didn't he realize he was spoiling her fun? She put her hands over her eyes, but she kept seeing him, with that unhappy look. Of course he looked unhappy; he hated to be with a birdbrain like Doreen, no question about it. But if he knew that she was not just dumb but terrible, if he could be made to understand that. . . . She sat straighter, as the taxi went past the BOUTIQUE FOR FINE FURS, the ART SHOP, the DELICATESSEN. She didn't mind leaving Tony tonight, she was furious at him, it served him right for the way he'd been acting. But to leave him with someone as terrible as Doreen.

If she had just been able to explain to him. Or if there had been someone else to give the explanation. Someone beside herself or, of course, Martin, who was dead, who knew how terrible Doreen really was. The taxi went by Lawson's —blue dresses in the window—and she thought: There *is* someone else. Mrs. Merimee knew.

The poor thing, my heart breaks for her—Mrs. Merimee had been signaling her knowledge. Dislike for Doreen had been implicit in that stony expression, in the two dollar bills outstretched on a disdainful palm, even in the gratuitous query:

Is she a friend of yours? But Jane Bassett had noticed none
of it. Wrapped up in her own injured pride, fresh from the
experience of being patronized by foolishness from a ladder in
a powder room, or insults flung lightly through an open door,
she had not seen that Mrs. Merimee's refusal to give money
might not be part of that casual negligence at all; it might be
in a very different category.

She saw it now; she spoke to the driver. "Not the station
after all. I changed my mind."

He looked at her with elaborate patience. Women passen-
gers: always more trouble than they were worth. "Soon as you
decide, lady, let me know."

She had decided. She had fully decided, even though it was
the worst time for an unsolicited visit: someone like Mrs.
Merimee would be getting dressed, or giving final orders about
a dinner party, or doing whatever was done in that kind of
house late on a Saturday afternoon. She leaned forward again.
No, she didn't care if they missed the six-twenty-five, she quite
understood, if he'd drive along Woodbine she would show him
where to stop.

18

It was the worst hour for an unsolicited visit, Tony thought. Dinner time—almost dinner time, anyhow, in a house with young children, which was what Steve Slocum had. And it was all his own fault; he could have been here as soon as Sheila gave the signal; who said he must spend the afternoon brooding, engulfed in misery, debating with himself as he walked unseeing through the festive brightness of a Saturday afternoon?

On and on the debate had gone. Why investigate further, you've lost Jane anyhow? . . . I still have to get the whole story, I want to know. . . . Big laugh: you think Steve Slocum is going to come across with any story, whole or otherwise? . . . He thinks I'm the most intelligent teacher in the school. Superlative. . . . Makes it better sport. A superlative teacher who acts like an idiot, exposes his own vulnerability—for someone like Steve what could be more fun?

He was here; they might be looking out the window. A man whose vulnerability was exposed, he rang the bell of the house which had a back yard adjoining the supermarket, a front one curtailed by a power station. "Well, Tony, hello." Steve was at the door. "Don't mind coming into the kitchen, do you? I don't think you know Eleanor. My wife. If you can see her under all this shampoo."

What he saw was a bent-over figure with hands clutching the sink and head doused in it—a muffled greeting came from her, a dubious one from him.

"Sit over there—that uncomfortable chair. . . . You're right, it's a terrible time to come, but sit anyhow, tomorrow will be just as bad. Tomorrow she'll be wanting her hair washed all over again."

An indignant dissent from that imprisoned figure—as he talked, Steve went on rubbing in soap, which was in clouds over her head and neck.

"She's a nut about her hair. Demented. She doesn't clean the dishes, and she lets the kids run around barefoot, and she hasn't swept the floor in a week—look, you can see the dirt all over—but she must have her hair washed every five days." The soaping was finished—with expert fingers he started to rinse. "If she had any other sensational features. Eleanor, hold still. Terrific eyes, say, or a Grecian nose. But no. When she was three years old, they told her about her glorious hair and that did it. She's hooked on these auburn tresses. Here, for God's sake, take this towel. You're dripping over everything."

She took the towel, wrapped it around her head, groaned with the pain of straightening after so long in a bent position, and turned to give her husband a look. It was an adoring one. "Steve, you're impossible," she said lovingly.

"Well, take your wet crowning glory and get out. Tony is very busy and conscientious, he wouldn't visit me late on a Saturday afternoon unless he had something absolutely vital to talk about."

The adoring look turned into a complacent smile—Steve was teasing her the way he teased everyone, and obviously she loved it. A contented woman, she padded out in her damp smock, her drenched hair, her bare feet. Some of the water dripped from the towel—he felt it as he leaned forward across the kitchen table.

"It is vital. Otherwise I wouldn't come barging in. The fact is—Steve, please tell me why Doreen came to see you the day before Martin died."

Steve made a sweeping gesture of disavowal. "Tony, I wish you wouldn't mention this where my wife can hear. I told you Doreen's a cute little—"

"I know. Cute little nitwit, if you had your choice you wouldn't give her the time of day."

"I can't betray professional confidences, you ought to know that."

It was the typical sparring—cynical, edgy, false. Now it was started, they could string it out indefinitely. Ethics, Steve would murmur with gravely specious piety, and, Just routine curiosity, he would deprecatingly say, and after ten minutes he would be where he had been before except a little worse: Steve would have more to bait him about as they got out of their cars in the parking lot.

He looked at the floor in front of the sink; marks of a woman's feet were distinct on the linoleum. She must still be wet—a child had been crying when she went out, and the crying had by now turned into the intermittent, indolent kind of sobs which meant that comfort was being not just administered but enjoyed. When they were rid of the inopportune guest who had just barged in, Steve would be in there too— this was not the kind of family where a child was left crying for long.

"Steve, I have to know about Doreen. Otherwise, things at home . . . my own marriage . . ."

"That pretty girl—what's her name? Jane?—something wrong in that department?"

"Worse than wrong. Shaky, you might say. Tottering." Despite the cravenly flippant words, he knew some of the earnestness must be apparent. Or perhaps Steve was skilled at reading behind flippancy—the hand that had been playing absently with an empty shampoo bottle put it down. "It's because of Doreen. She's done it," he went on.

"You mean you fell for that little—"

"God, no—nothing like that. But she's around. A fixture. I didn't realize when I started helping her . . . taking care of her."

Steve stood up and turned off the water, which nonetheless kept dripping. "Why would any man in his right mind think he had to take care of Doreen Cobden?"

He drew a breath. For a month he had evaded saying it, Steve Slocum was surely the last person to whom he had expected to say it, he needed the utmost concentration on Sheila's words to have the strength to say it. "I took Martin's job."

"How d'you figure that?"

"He wanted to be department head. For years he took it for granted the job would be his. So naturally, when he didn't get it . . ."

"You poor sap. Is that the burden you've been carrying around all this time?"

"Something made him commit suicide. I know that wasn't the whole reason, of course, it couldn't be. But it must have been part of it."

It was Steve's turn to hesitate, his eyes fixed on the wet linoleum—were those prints of a woman's bare feet able to convey a message to everyone? "You serious about all this— trouble between you and your wife?"

He didn't answer; it was not, obviously, a question; it was part of the deliberation, weighing of factors, going on inside a congenitally deliberate man. Above the sound of both their breathing was the drip of water—someone ought to put in a new washer, he thought. "Well, of course Martin didn't commit suicide," Steve said at last.

He looked up—he felt not so much surprise as relief; it was like hearing the confirmation of some faith, some wholly mystical fervor, that had sustained him all along. "What makes you think that?"

"I don't think, I know. I wouldn't say it if I didn't know." In Steve's tone was a reminder, for an instant, of the man who could find your weak spots and have a high old time with them. "Martin was not the suicidal kind. He was erratic, and he sometimes showed lousy judgment, and he was bored silly with his job, but he was not remotely in the kind of depression that leads to suicide. Far from it. In fact, he had lately found out that he had a hell of a lot to live for."

He rubbed his hand along the table. Was this all it was going to be: a school psychologist's hunch, delivered with the testy air of authority that passes for dogma? "Then you think—"

"Stop saying 'think.' I'm giving you the truth. Doreen was the one."

"I see."

"Not yet, you don't, but you will. She'd tried to commit suicide twice before. Twice, that is, that I know of—God knows how many other attempts there were that Martin hushed up. There's only one person who could have put cyanide into that glass, and only one reason she had for doing it."

"What happened those other two times?" ·

"Once she cut her wrist. A bad cut, but not so bad they couldn't fix her up at the hospital, dispatch her home the next morning with some stitches."

"There's this redheaded nurse," he said absurdly.

"Those nurses—they know which side is up. Catch them falling for some phony story about a slippery bread knife."

"What happened the other time?"

Steve leaned forward, listening, but it was all right: that shriek from the other room was one of delight—it was followed by a melodious peal of adult laughter. She does have some beautiful attribute besides her hair, he thought.

"Something with sleeping pills," Steve said. "Again, enough to get Martin good and scared, not too many for a doctor to handle easily."

"That was the point—to scare Martin?"

"With someone like Doreen it usually is. Watch out for little me or I'll hurt myself and you'll be sorry. Standard in these suicide attempts."

"Suppose the joke's on her and it's more than just an attempt? I mean, suppose she really killed herself. It could happen."

"Not the careful way Doreen planned things, it couldn't. She didn't make a move unless she knew damn well there was no danger, someone would be around to pick up the pieces."

Someone: suddenly Martin's presence had moved in on them. Was it after bringing a wife back from the hospital with a bandage around her wrist that he had taken on permanently that cynical look? Was it during the bout with sleeping pills that he decided the hell with fixing the posters that were meant for visual aids on the wall?

"It's the way her type always operates," Steve said. "They try suicide, all right, but they have the timetable down pat, so some poor sucker is there in the nick of time to bind the wound or pump the stomach or clean up whatever other damage is done. Some fellow who'll feel ashamed he was mean before, and know he has to be solicitous ever after—they see to that."

Steve moved restlessly; two phone books were on the seat of his chair, a contraption that must be arranged for some child not yet high enough to reach the table. He frowned at the books, as though wondering what they were doing there, but he didn't bother to move them. "There wasn't supposed to be any danger this time either. She'd have drunk two or three sips of that stuff at just six-fifteen, and then waited for Martin to get off the train at six-eighteen, the way he always did, and be on hand in his own kitchen ten minutes later."

"She wasn't even in the apartment when Martin got there."

"The schedule got a little mixed up—she didn't plan on a neighbor having labor pains. But I bet if you check with that family across the hall, you'll find that when they called her she was in her kitchen, she had the drink all fixed, she was ready to gulp it down. Or as much of it, anyhow, as she needed to create her effect."

She could have refused to babysit, he started to say and didn't—the boisterous pressures of that family crowded in. He saw the child making a bicycle route out of the living-room rug, and, watching from the sides, the silent ones who of course would not stay silent long, and, inside, that composed girl with the high forehead, the knowing eyes. Lorie, he remembered. Lorie reaching for the talcum, moving a wash cloth gently across a year-old child, cajoling the inept baby sitter into believing the myth of her own usefulness—a girl like that would remember exactly what happened before Doreen came.

Then that tableau dissolved, and in its place was a figure with hands dangling under a table, a face twisted from convulsion. "Maybe she wanted Martin to drink that poison," he said slowly. "It was not an accident at all."

"You suggesting murder?" Steve said.

Murder: unseemly even to pronounce it in this kitchen where a coloring book was open on the floor, corn flakes were spilled across the counter, a half-eaten cookie lay at the other end of the table beside a half-drunk glass of milk. "It's possible."

"Theoretically, yes. But believe me, Tony, what I'm telling you is the truth. Murder doesn't fit with Doreen. With what we know about her character."

They were still in the territory of hunches, conjecture. Skilled conjecture, maybe, but conjecture all the same. "Maybe for an hour she stepped out of character."

"That wasn't her kind of aberration. She didn't want Martin dead—she wanted him alive to take care of her, be her meal ticket. She just had to remind him from time to time what a frail little bundle she was."

"Anyone that unstable—" he began, and realized from the look on Steve's face, the suddenly taut expression, that what was about to come was the critical revelation, and that it wouldn't be produced with any less pain or unease than he, Tony, had felt about exposing his own secret ten minutes ago. "The reason I know she planned to kill herself is she told me. This show had been planned in advance. She gave me warning."

He sat motionless. "That day in your office?"

"That day in my office. It was three-thirty—Angie had it on the button—and a girl with an appointment was outside in the hall. But I couldn't let her in because of Doreen. Doreen was crying—those obliging tears." Only the faint quiver in Steve's voice showed what this cost him. "'I'll kill myself,' she told me. 'If Martin goes ahead with this, he'll be responsible for my life.'"

For a second all he could picture was that girl waiting outside the small office. It was hard enough for them to make the appointment with Mr. Slocum—once there, they shouldn't have to wait. She would stand uncomfortably, moving her books from side to side, lowering her eyes when a crowd of students walked past. Or did she decide not to wait after all, when that promised door didn't open did she take her unresolved problems, her adolescent fears, and go down with a new grievance to her locker?

"What was Martin planning to go ahead with?"

Steve looked for a second at the coloring book—pink Indians were smoking in front of a blue-striped tepee. "There was another woman, he wanted a divorce."

"I'm surprised it didn't happen before."

"Oh, she always knew how he felt. That's what those other scares were about: to get him back in line."

"Who was the other woman?" he said slowly.

"I don't think Doreen knew, and if she did, she didn't tell me. But she did know he wasn't kidding around, she had to move fast."

"How come she spoke to you?"

"She knew me fairly well—Martin had sent her in a couple of times before. This time the visit was her idea. She wanted me to use my influence with Martin, get him to change his mind."

"Did you try?"

"Listen, I *liked* that guy," Steve said in all the answer that was needed.

"I liked him too." His hand reached out, crumbled the cookie. "This other woman—was it something sudden, did you gather?"

"Just the opposite. He told Doreen he'd been seeing her all year, he was definite, he wouldn't change his mind."

All year . . . again Angie had been the one to hit it first: Last thing Martin would do with a Tuesday or Thursday afternoon was listen to some idiot professor of education. "He had an excuse for getting away two afternoons a week. I suppose he was meeting her."

"I certainly hope so." It was a minor comfort: out of the rigorously overseen week, the supervised schedule, a few clandestine hours devoted to pleasure.

"I asked Doreen, but if she had any guesses about his destination, she wasn't letting on to me."

"Why should she? She sized you up right: the honorable friend, all tied up in guilt." For an instant it was the old Steve on the other side of the table, the amused tone and wily glance trained in the exploitation of someone else's weakness. "She wanted to keep you tied up. But once you start finding out things, the picnic ends. The poor little widow won't seem quite so helpless."

"And I guess Martin meant it about being department head for just a year. Till he got his divorce—he'd need that year here under his belt to get him settled."

"Glad you have everything worked out, Tony."

But it was not quite worked out. He looked toward the door; quiet in that other part of the house, but the woman with the celebrated hair, the melodious laugh, must want to come back in and start supper. When can I get my coloring book, a child would say—a whole family wishing the uninvited company would take himself off. "If you knew all this, if you've known it all along, why didn't you say so?"

"Same reason you kept your mouth shut about having applied for department head over Martin. Self-protection."

"I don't get it."

"Think back to that week when Martin died. I was coming up for a new job with the school board just the way you were. They were meeting Thursday; on Monday night, Martin was dead. Suppose I'd told the truth: I know he didn't commit suicide because his wife told me she was going to, only I didn't take her seriously, I laughed her off. . . . Can't you just hear it?"

He said nothing. He sat upright at the kitchen table.

"I know what you're thinking. I could have talked my way out of it. All the reasonable explanations: it sounded like a phony threat, she'd made phony threats before, I was justified in thinking this threat wasn't any less phony than the others. I had a case—absolutely right." It was another side to Steve: one agonizing, appealing, on the defensive. "Okay, my professional judgment was faultless, but try to explain about faultless professional judgment to a school board. Especially try to explain it when a colleague is dead."

"All this time, letting everyone think Martin committed suicide . . ." Letting me think it, was what he meant.

"Guidance Director—I wanted that extra money. Needed it. Look around this house and you'll see why. . . . All right, maybe I could have convinced them. But maybe not. Just one person at a board meeting who voices misgivings—all you need to swing a vote against you."

"Once you had the job, you could have—"

"What for, Tony? Martin was dead—not all the truth in the world could bring him back to life. And I couldn't prove anything. As you say, it could have happened some other way. It damn well didn't, but it could have. There's nothing definite in the picture—not even the kind of hard fact that would bring that little conniver up before a judge. All I could do by talking was make trouble for myself."

There was one more question; drawing a breath, he put it fast. "Why did you ask me about knowing them when they lived on Rivers Street?"

"I wanted to see how much you knew—if Martin had confided in you about Doreen's suicidal habits. No use my clamming up if you were going to hand out the whole story. But it was clear Martin's evasiveness went all the way: you didn't know a thing about him outside school. Not even where they'd lived. Didn't live."

So it was as simple as that: all those lugubrious thoughts, and a fellow faculty member had just been looking ahead, taking some elementary precautions to spare himself embarrassment later on. Steve may have guessed how much discomfort he had caused—when he spoke again, his voice was gentle. "I'd ask you to stay for dinner. Hamburgers, I think Eleanor said—she cooks the way she cleans. But maybe you want to get home to that pretty wife."

He pushed back his chair, walked carefully around the coloring book, the dripping sink. "I do want to get home. But thanks anyhow." Because what was the use of explaining that all these revelations came too late. His pretty wife had offhandedly done some revealing on her own, she must already be on her way with her perfect hairdo, her refurbished dress, her newly acknowledged plans?

19

"But I have to see her, it's important."

"Mrs. Merimee is busy."

"Just five minutes. If you'd tell her Mrs. Bassett . . ." The maid's disapproval passed over her, and she realized how she must look. One didn't come unannounced to this house on a Saturday night. One certainly didn't come wearing a black satin evening dress, silver shoes. She swayed a little. That grandiose notion had seemed so heroic, so daring: to find out the crucial fact that was going to end the trouble between her and her husband. But crucial facts did not emerge from conversations that were impromptu, forced. Besides, even assuming Mrs. Merimee knew something derogatory about Doreen, what good would it do? She had already derogated Doreen herself, told Tony plenty—what more could be accomplished from the testimony of one who had probably met Doreen at a school function, had the intelligence to dislike her.

"Never mind. I shouldn't have come."

"Is it that important?" Mrs. Merimee was on the stairs—how much of the conversation had she heard?

"I didn't mean to barge in."

"I assume you want more money for Mrs. Cobden."

"Well, I—"

"Come in a minute. In here."

She followed the woman into an enormous living room. Feeling dwarfed, conspicuous, she waded timorously into her opening speech. "Mrs. Merimee, actually it's not money at all—"

"I should have given you more yesterday. I was busy."

"But I'm trying to tell you, I don't care about the money, it isn't that."

"Lovely of you to do this, I'm sure. Generous. All you busy people." She was trying to tell, but it came over her that Mrs. Merimee was not trying to listen.

"I'm not being lovely at all, that's not why—"

"If there is a collection, I wouldn't want poor Mrs. Cobden to—"

"Mrs. Cobden can drop dead," she said shrilly.

"Well, she won't, of course." Mrs. Merimee went over to the desk. "That type never does."

"What do you mean, that type?"

"Mrs. Bassett, I don't have endless time and I'm sure you don't either. Now. How do you want the check made out?"

"Please tell me what you know about her, I beg you."

"A hundred dollars, will that be—"

"You must believe me." Was it the size of the room making her voice thin, her words hollow? "I didn't come for money. I wouldn't take the money if you gave it."

Mrs. Merimee lay her pen on the leather desk top; she was listening.

"All I want—I thought if you could tell me about Mrs. Cobden. I wouldn't ask if it weren't important. I would never have come."

That good-looking face stared attentively. "I don't know Mrs. Cobden. I never met her."

"But you said—"

"I wouldn't recognize her if I passed her on the street."

"You gave me to understand—"

"For all I know I was next to her today in a store. I haven't the faintest idea what she looks like."

She felt suddenly dizzy; when she put out her hand, all she felt was the curve of the piano.

"Sorry to disappoint you, but now you understand."

She couldn't speak; her hand still searched for something to grip.

"You must be late," the woman said, though not unkindly. "What time is your party?"

"Party? . . . Oh, this." She looked down at the unaccustomed folds of satin around her ankles; there was a rip in the skirt; getting in or out of the taxi, she must have stuck her heel through the hastily turned-up hem.

". . . needle and thread."

She lifted her dazed head.

"I can give you needle and thread," the woman repeated gently. "That is, if you're not in a terrible rush. Just twenty to seven."

Twenty to seven. Alan would not yet have started. He would know to a split second the time required to get to the station; he would not come late, but he wouldn't stand around for a single extra minute either in the vicinity of the lower-level information booth.

"Sometimes if you fix a tear before it gets any worse."

She kicked vaguely at the skirt; the tear disappeared in the satin folds. "Doesn't matter."

"Mrs. Bassett, you don't look very—would you like a drink? Some coffee?"

Did it all show on her face? "Coffee would be wonderful." A bell must have been rung, an order given—when she sat, she was conscious of the clink of cups.

"This terrible heat. Unusual for this time of year, maybe that's why it affects us more." It wasn't heat making her dizzy, and Mrs. Merimee must have guessed it wasn't. Was it to make up for former incivility that this effort was being made? Or was this woman automatically nice on any subject except money for Doreen, was niceness a natural manner? She bent over her cup—a cozy languor had replaced the faintness.

"I guess I was rushing too much."

"You have a baby, don't you? Always a rush, leaving them at this time of night. All those last-minute orders."

"Our baby sitter is very conscientious. Darling. But you have to say everything three times."

"Don't I remember that stage? Seventeen years ago, but I

remember. More coffee?" Mrs. Merimee picked up her own cup. Under the conventional, sunburnt, long-legged good grooming, there was something else that added beauty. A sympathetic look? A discerning one? Or was it both these, plus the hint of an inner sadness that made them possible? "Your child was sick when she was born, wasn't she?"

"Not exactly sick. Something twisted. They had to operate when she was three days old."

"We had trouble, too, with Bert. Very different—a skin ailment—but I know what it was like. That business of leaving him in the hospital. Going home without a baby."

That harrowing period was back. "Some days I'd look at the empty crib and think I might as well give it away. Obviously my own child would never use it," Jane said.

"The worst thing is, your own child is a stranger. You left him before you had a chance to know him."

"I thought something was wrong with me. When they'd hold up this creature on the other side of the glass, I had no maternal feelings. Took weeks of having her home."

"Oh, you're so right. Weeks and weeks." A smile, shyly comfortable, went both ways across the coffee table. You'll be talking to those women, Linda had said, but what she had in mind was a conversation about sculpture, gardens, yachts, with the stylish allusions that would bear repeating. There would be nothing to repeat out of this, as she sat tomorrow with Linda in the playground. In fact, it was the kind of talk she might be having with Linda: one in which needle and thread were proffered, disease symptoms exchanged, acknowledgments made about not loving unknown babies.

Then she looked up. Mrs. Merimee had responded tactfully to her guest's unhappiness, but how did she get the information for this response? How did she know Betsy had been sick at birth? Or, in fact, that Betsy existed at all? Her son had been in Martin's eleventh-grade class, but that tenuous link couldn't begin to explain it.

She put down her cup. "I wonder how you happen to know—"

"I mustn't keep you any longer." Mrs. Merimee was standing. "Since you're going to a party."

Of course: that mythical party which, in this well-bred house, was all that could account for her outfit. She looked again at her dress—for a relaxed second, she had forgotten.

"You feel better now, don't you?"

"I feel fine."

"I'll call you a taxi. Which do you use?"

"I don't know. Standard. Blue Bird—any one."

"Afraid I kept you too long." Mrs. Merimee was at the door. "Your husband will be waiting."

She brushed a crumb off her dress. "I guess so."

"He's a wonderful teacher—everyone says so. I'm sorry Bert didn't have him."

She nodded. I feel fine, she had said, but it wasn't true—that heaviness again assaulted her head. Voices sounded beyond the door; she was conscious of the efficiency with which this household would work. The taxi would already be on its way—where to, the driver would say before she had even settled herself into the seat.

Mrs. Merimee was watching her. "Don't be anxious. They tell you they'll be right there, five minutes at most, but sometimes it's closer to fifteen."

"That's all right." The movies—how would that be for a destination? Sitting in the anonymous dark, you could have solitude, immunity from talk. She would look ridiculous, of course—someone in evening clothes going into the Stoney-crest Cinema; she would attract the attention of the teen-agers lined up in their faded jeans and colored shirts. But they wouldn't recognize her; Tony's pupils would have no way of knowing that the ludicrous figure two rows from the back was married to the wonderful Mr. Bassett.

Tony's pupils wouldn't know her, and neither would their parents. But here was Mrs. Merimee knowing about Tony's wife, and Tony's wife's baby, and also Martin's wife, whom she claimed never to have met. Knowing even about that time of anxiety and sickness when only Martin's help had kept Tony going in school.

". . . sometimes busy, this time of night— There it is now."

There it must be—that single imperious honk. The driver, leaning out, would smell the fragrance from unseen flowers. Her hands and feet must have performed prescribed motions —she was across the room, she was at the door.

"Thank you very much for the coffee."

"It was nice to meet you."

"I do appreciate—"

"Mrs. Bassett, what's the matter?"

"Nothing."

"You can't meet your husband looking like that, you have to stop crying before you—"

"I'm not meeting him. He's with Doreen Cobden. He's out with her."

Mrs. Merimee picked up a crumpled napkin and put it down. "I'm sure any minute he'll be—"

"He was with her yesterday. He'll be with her tomorrow. He thinks he has to take care of her." She stopped, but Mrs. Merimee had said nothing; that stifled noise was one of her own sobs. "Please tell me what you know about Doreen. Please. If I could tell my husband, and get him back. . . ."

There was no answer, but how could there be—she was alone in the room; outside, she heard the scrape of tire on gravel. Taxis didn't go till someone paid them, did they? Was it a sign? Dimly, she heard the living-room doors being closed, tested, closed firmly again—then Mrs. Merimee was beside her.

"Don't let her get your husband."

"He wants to protect her. He thinks he's responsible for her."

"They all do. Till they figure out the facts. Only then it's too late."

"I don't—" But suddenly she did understand; her tears stopped, abashed, before the harshness of sudden understanding. She looked around this room with its couches, its over-size chairs, its grand piano—all objects too big for a woman living alone—and then she looked at the grief-stricken face of the woman herself. A woman who had the exact measure of Doreen's slyness, and the exact amount of revulsion toward it, and could only have acquired them both the same way she had acquired her information about everything connected with the school.

Why, she's the one who ought to be crying. The one who lost something. "I'm terribly sorry. I didn't realize."

"It's all right."

"Martin was wonderful, wasn't he?"

"Yes."

"I'm sorry I asked all those questions. I was an idiot. I should have guessed."

"No one else guessed, why should you?" Mrs. Merimee paused, but only to make sure the footsteps outside the room didn't mean any intrusion within it. "Not one person ever guessed. Not for a year."

"That's how long you—"

"More than a year. But we didn't become—we didn't start meeting till last fall. Every Tuesday and Thursday afternoon. I had some committee meetings—it's easy for someone like me to invent committee meetings in New York—and he had those Education courses teachers are supposed to take, and there we were." For a second the woman smiled; it was the contrast between that smile and the expression that closed it off that made her realize how difficult this was. I'm sorry, Jane kept wanting to say. I'm terribly sorry. . . .

"I never meant to probe," she said instead.

"You have to get your husband back. We can't let Doreen have him. Now, where were we?"

"Tuesday and Thursday afternoons . . ." She blew her nose; the frailty of her own emotion struck her again.

"Two whole afternoons a week, in a city where no one knew us, no one was likely to see us."

"Was that so important? That no one should see you?"

Mrs. Merimee took a step, stopped, moved forward again. "See this picture? It's Bert. My son."

"I know about him—Tony told me. He's a very nice boy."

"He writes poetry. In the school magazine—I guess you don't see it—there was something last month. About a wave—an ambivalent wave." Ambivalent . . . the word hung in the quiet room. "And he is nice, he really is. But last year he wasn't so nice, you had to like him an awful lot to find anything nice about him. And the year before that, when his father died." Again that pause. "I mean, the kind of trouble he was in. . . . Yours is still a baby, Mrs. Bassett. You don't know how it can be. They can come out of a house like this, and have all the love in the world, and still, when you're called to the police station at three o'clock some morning . . ."

"I know it happens," she said quickly.

"You think, not my sixteen-year-old they're talking about, it can't be. . . . Anyhow, he was lucky—some wonderful people around to help. A guidance counselor at school. A doctor. And his eleventh-grade English teacher."

"Martin . . ."

"It was the first time since his father died—someone he didn't mind talking to. He wanted to talk to. He said maybe he'd hang around school for another month."

They can go either way—for a second it was Tony's voice Jane was hearing.

"A conference every few weeks with Bert's teacher—that's how it started," Bert's mother said simply.

"I see." It was easy to see: the good-looking, lonely, intelligent woman, the bright, cynical teacher who went home at night to a birdbrain.

"And Bert . . . well, you know about him. He's graduating this month. He'll start college in the fall. We were going to tell him next Thanksgiving."

"Tell him?"

"You don't think we were going to keep up this sordid business forever, do you? The meetings in hotel rooms. The makeshift excuses. Martin and I—we were going to get married," her voice said into the folds of curtain.

I'm sorry. I'm really sorry—how much longer must the refrain go uselessly on? "But if you could tell a boy next year? . . ."

"Next year he'll be a college freshman. This year he's an adolescent at home with his mother. There's a big difference. At least, the doctors told me there was a big difference. Get him through high school, don't make any changes, see that he's secure enough to apply for college—that was their advice and I had to follow it. After that, they said, he could take anything."

Really sorry . . .

"The only thing we didn't realize was how she would take it. Or, rather, not take it."

"Doreen . . ." Even not hearing, she would have known. What other subject could cause the small shudder, the icy voice—for a second, Mrs. Merimee was again the woman who had turned on a stranger with haughty inscrutability on her own front lawn.

"She wasn't surprised. For all her hysterical fusses, she had no illusions; she knew what he thought about the marriage. But this time he was definite. Not a tentative hint but a settled timetable. He wanted a divorce this summer."

"Did she know who you were?"

"She didn't have to. It was enough if she knew that farce of a marriage was over."

"It's a wonder she got him to stick with her that long," she said.

"He felt guilty," Mrs. Merimee said bitterly. "She fell when they were mountain climbing; he thought it was his fault. And when it left her injured, she couldn't have children—"

"Is that what she told him?"

"For four years she wouldn't let him forget it," the woman said.

She spoke slowly. "Doreen *could* have had children—I just found out. She didn't want to. She had this convenient myth —she could keep her husband and still have her freedom."

Then the woman turned, she saw that ravaged face—what was the point of going over it? "What about that business of teaching for one more year?" Jane asked.

"We were going to move, we didn't want to keep living here. But he couldn't live entirely on my money either—not Martin. He needed one more year in Stoneycrest while the divorce went through. And he'd have liked to be department head during that year. Naturally."

How natural it all was, when you had the key. All those speculative hours during which she and Tony had made the wild guesses, seized on the dubious suppositions. "Martin was always so secretive," she murmured.

"It was all going to stop being secret. Very soon it was going to stop. Dear God, the years that stretched before us." Then, as if disavowing emotion, ending it, Mrs. Merimee sat in a chair like any hostess facing her guest. "Till she killed him," her hostess' voice unemphatically said.

Don't tremble. You expected this. In your heart it was what you expected, what kept you going during all the trouble with Tony, what led you to come here this evening.

"You didn't think Martin would commit suicide, did you? He was dreaming about the future. He was just going to start to live."

She was the one at the window now, peering out at a lawn that stretched to the water. She expected this in the sense that she had felt them moving toward it, and yet there were the facts that had made it seem impossible, blocked it.

"Why would Doreen kill her husband when it left her penniless."

"The poor little widow—that's what she has you thinking. You can save your sympathy," Mrs. Merimee said through tight lips. "Her mother is very comfortably fixed. I don't mean health—that rest home she's in is really for terminal diseases; she can't live more than another few months—but money is no problem. Your widow will have as much from her mother's estate as she ever got from a teacher's salary."

They had been stinting themselves, doling out the dollar bills. Then she realized there had been no one at the funeral or any other place to set them straight. "What about that letter Martin wrote?"

The woman turned with great scorn. "I did read in the papers that there was a letter. What did it say?"

"'When you're alone, I want you to live in Vermont; it will be better for you up there.'"

"That was Martin. Considerate. He couldn't wait to be rid of her, but he had to be kind to her too. He told me he'd try to put some things in writing. Because you couldn't talk to her. She simply would not listen."

That pushy little figure, with her calculated inattentiveness, her talent for misunderstanding.

"She wouldn't listen, but I guess after all, she did. She said, 'If I can't have you, I'll make sure some other woman doesn't either!'"

"That's what Doreen said?"

"I was terrified when Martin told me. I begged him to be careful. But he laughed it off. He said she was the kind to make empty threats, she'd been doing it for years." Mrs. Merimee stared straight ahead, past the picture of her son, the glossy table tops. "Except this threat wasn't so empty. She carried it off."

Past the closed door, she could hear the hum of an electric mixer—someone would be whipping cream, making sauce. In fifteen minutes this woman would be expected to sit down opposite her son, make interested conversation about his day, comment graciously about the meal.

"But Martin took that drink himself. No one forced him. Doreen wasn't even around."

"Check with that family across the hall. I bet you'll find she made that drink—something she knew he liked—and put the poison in it, and then got herself called away a few strategic minutes before she expected him home. Just ask them —it'll turn out that she offered to go over there. She didn't wait to be asked—there was nothing accidental about this. She heard the commotion in that apartment, and she realized it was her big chance, and she grabbed it. Oh, she was very clever, the poor little widow."

"What you're saying is . . . murder. You think Doreen murdered him."

"I don't think," Mrs. Merimee said coldly. "I'm telling you the truth. You wanted to know about Doreen Cobden, and I'm telling you. She killed him. She cold-bloodedly planned to kill her husband, and she did."

"But if you knew all this—"

"Why didn't I make it public? Is that what you're asking?"

"Please forgive me. I know this is terrible for you."

"It is terrible," that implacable voice agreed. "But it could be even worse. You know what a reporter would find, don't you? The hotel on East Fifty-second Street where we always had the same room. The ride home on separate trains. The little stratagem because someone once saw us together on the street. Details like that . . . all right to read about, maybe, if you're thirty. Twenty, even. But Bert is seventeen. A seventeen-year-old boy on the borderline of being disturbed—do you know what it might do to him? That kind of record of shabby lying about his mother and his favorite teacher?"

Unanswerable, the question accosted her. "Besides, the fact is, I couldn't prove it. That woman murdered Martin, she planned to murder him, she had every reason to murder him —I know exactly what happened, but in the end all I could do was point suspicion at her. I couldn't get her in jail. I couldn't even be sure of getting her punished."

She was silent.

"But I *will* speak up now—"

"What do you mean?"

"I thought I was alone in all this. Doreen was finished, I took for granted—she'd done all the damage she could. But if she's still making trouble for you and your husband—"

You can't start crying again. This woman isn't crying, and

you can't indulge yourself either. "You don't have to tell anything. If Tony just knows definitely that Martin didn't commit
suicide, if I have your permission to tell him that."

"You can tell him anything to keep him from that woman."

20

Lorie sat on the edge of the bed, or, rather, on that small part of it not damp from the baby's bath. "Sure I'll tell you anything," she said.

"Terrible time to bother you."

"That's okay." It was not polite to stare, but how could you help it when your visitor had not only appeared suddenly at the door of your room, but was wearing, inexplicably, a black evening dress.

"You're an angel to help me."

"It's okay," she said again. But she didn't feel angelic; she knew exactly how vulnerable she was; at fourteen, you answered questions out of expediency. Adults had a way not only of discovering the facts you had withheld from them, but of considering themselves entitled to the reasons for your withholding. Why didn't you want to tell us, Lorie?—that kind of question could make more complications than any answer you gave.

And in a family like this, she had too many complications already. Especially she had them on a Saturday evening. This Saturday had been no better or worse than usual. A sponge bath for the baby—who of course was no longer the baby—and a fight with Mary and Ellen, who shared this room but better stay away from her shelves, and a dash to the library, and, when this lady in evening clothes turned up, the ready assumption from her mother of a child's availability. In fact, her mother hadn't even bothered to find out why the visitor was here; it was enough, at this hour when three crises were going on at once, that she herself wasn't wanted, someone else's attention was being sought.

She leaned back on the bed. "Please try to remember," the lady was saying. "I know it happened more than a month ago, but please. It was the night your mother went to the hospital to have a baby. Remember that?"

She nodded, while her visitor sat, stood nervously, sat again. Though her dress showed a satisfying amount of shoulder and bosom, she didn't in the least resemble the standard pictures of people in evening clothes. In these, the models always had an air of stately detachment—nothing detached about this lady with her rumpled hair, her stained shoes, her worried look. Even her dress was torn—a long rip up one side of the satin skirt.

At the same time, she was not bad looking at all. In fact, she would be pretty if she would put on lipstick, run a comb through that tangled hair—with a little effort, she could hold her own with any of the models.

"You do remember, don't you?"

"I guess so."

"It must have been about six o'clock. Your mother had to leave in a hurry. She must have started to . . . she started . . ."

"She's supposed to go to the hospital when the pains are five minutes apart." Dispassionate, she interposed this piece of the familiar routine.

"I see." Briefly, the visitor smiled. "Now, try to think back. There must have been all that excitement—your mother rushing to pack her clothes, and the younger children running around, and maybe some of them crying."

"Prissy cried."

"You do remember, then."

"She always cries. She's crying right now." It was true; over the sound of children's voices in the next room came the thin wail of this sixth of nine children who cried because her shoe-lace broke, her doll looked sad, life generally assumed menacing proportions.

"That afternoon, then. That special afternoon." Her visitor

tugged at memory, steering it. "It was terribly hot that day—people would naturally leave their doors open." For a second they both looked around this room; the door was closed to keep out the sound of Robert and Henry's fighting, Prissy's crying, Mary's orders to someone to give back her puzzle. "And Mrs. Cobden was here. Baby sitting. You remember that?"

She frowned. "We really don't need a baby sitter. I'm fourteen and a half. If there's anything at all—"

"Honey, I know. I really do." The lady looked as if she did; under the tousled hair she had, for a second, the expression of one who knew exactly how responsibility between herself, Lorie, and Mrs. Cobden had been allotted. "But that particular time, your parents gone for the whole night. Someone had to be here. Someone older. For after you'd gone to sleep."

Mollified, she waited.

"And what I want to know is, who suggested it? I mean, did your mother say, Get Mrs. Cobden to stay here? Or was Mrs. Cobden the one? Did she make the suggestion herself?"

"I really don't—"

"She could have heard all the noise and come over. After all, that terribly hot day."

She looked out the window. How could anyone remember the weather on any day a month before?

"With the doors open, and everyone screaming," her visitor's insistent voice explained. "Would have been so easy for someone from across the hall to just show up here." That pretty face, framed by the bare shoulders, turned its compelling look toward her. "Was that the way it happened? Mrs. Cobden coming over without being asked? Please try to remember. Please."

Actually, she was trying. Despite her disinterest in anything so remote, it was hard not to try in the face of this lady's agitation. Lorie leaned back, under the three shelves that were her special territory and Mary and Ellen better remember it if they knew what was good for them, and as she concentrated, the scene materialized. Or, rather, the standard household routine materialized, and you could superimpose on it any date at all. Six o'clock; what went on—what must have been going on—came readily to mind: Robert and Henry fighting, and Prissy crying, and her father looking for Lance, who was always lost, and Stanley begging to ride his bike in the living room; he wouldn't hurt anything if he just could ride in the living room. All quite ordinary; without any effort, she could see it. If she tried, she could also see what this lady had suggested, which was Mrs. Cobden in the doorway offering to help. She would be wearing one of those little-girl dresses with the scooped neck and puffed sleeves that might look better on Ellen, and she would fold and unfold her hands because she never seemed to know what to do with them, and she would speak a couple of times in that high-pitched voice, which for all its shrillness was unable to command attention when other noise was going on. Not a thing in the world to do, that shrill voice was saying, she'd be glad to stay with the children, they could count on her.

Lorie sat back. Mrs. Cobden offering herself as baby sitter —why not? She could remember perfectly, sliding the scene into that conjured-up evening as simply as she slid into the area in Mary's puzzle the jagged piece that plainly fit there. The only trouble was, she had remembered something quite different for the man who was here a little while ago. He had walked in as unexpectedly as this lady, and had been likewise delegated by her mother to talk with her, Lorie. He had even sat in that same position on Ellen's bed. "Try to remember," he had said. "That night your mother had the baby and Mrs. Cobden came to babysit. I was here for a few minutes. Remember?"

She was held by the serious look of his eyes, under the bushy eyebrows. He did look slightly familiar, now that he mentioned it.

"You were bathing the baby," he prompted her. "Mrs. Cobden was—um—helping you"—and from the hesitation in his voice, it was plain that he too had sized up the situation, he knew exactly who was doing what. "You were sponging the baby when I came in. Now do you remember?"

"Mr. Cobden died that night. We heard the ambulance. Lance saw the policeman."

"Yes." An impenetrable look veiled his eyes, and she understood that this questioning had in some way to do with that curious death. But he said nothing and the harshness slipped from his face just the way, that night, that grotesque procession Lance had told them about must have slipped through the hall, so by next morning there was only the brief presence of a single policeman to give any corroboration to Lance's story.

The man held her gaze. "What I meant was, can you remember what happened before Mrs. Cobden got here? When your mother realized she had to leave in a hurry, and someone was needed to stay with you children?"

"Well, it—"

"Someone went over to ask Mrs. Cobden. Someone must have—didn't they? How else would she know to come?" His questions carried you effortlessly along, like the questions of an algebra teacher she'd had last year. He would ask something, and guide your thoughts over unfamiliar ground, and then ask something else, and wait patiently for you to follow, and at the end you somehow found yourself with information you didn't have before. In the same way, the information was seeping in now.

"Was it you who went over? Your mother must have been busy, and you being the oldest—I'm just trying to reconstruct it."

She nodded, to show her compliance in the reconstruction.

"Just a matter of opening the door, going across the hall. Someone get Mrs. Cobden quickly, your mother might have said. Is that the way it was?"

"I guess so." Why not?—he made it as persuasive as the proofs in algebra.

"Now." He fixed her with that urgent look which was also flattering, made you feel not everyone would be up to these special feats of memory. "When you went to get Mrs. Cobden, was she sitting at her kitchen table? Was that where she was?"

She nodded again, letting the door to their apartment open in her mind, going past the clutter in the hall, following him into the Cobden apartment where, occasionally, they used to wander.

"Such terribly hot weather, everyone gets thirsty. Isn't that right?"

He was not only emphatic but anxious; thinking back under the force of his kindly and yet compelling gaze, she had found it easy to recall the scene. She could see the pink and green edging around the kitchen shelves, and the cookie cutters in that fancy arrangement on the wall, and the painted calendar beside the door, and she could also see Mrs. Cobden sitting there.

"Did she seem just about ready to take a drink? Something cool, with ice?"

How forceful he was! How distinctly he made it come to life! She certainly could picture it. There was the plastic ice bucket. There was one of those glasses with the gold-coin designs. There was Mrs. Cobden's hand on the glass. No, the glass was going down; Mrs. Cobden was saying, Of course she'd come if they needed her. She could remember very well, and she had told him so, and now, an hour later, she could just as well remember the scene which this visitor in a black satin dress was suggesting. Which way did it happen? Which of the versions was correct? She thought briefly of telling this visitor her dilemma, explaining the haze of distance which gave to each of these contradictory scenes equal plausibility, equal strength. But that would mean an explanation about the man who had come earlier—whatever was involved, it could only lead to more trouble. She had long ago found out that, with grown-ups, whereas it was expedient to answer their questions, it was equally important to give them nothing extra. Who started that fight, your mother would ask, and a snappy, one-word, over-simplified answer brought about a settlement of sorts within five minutes. Whereas a conscientious, labored, thoroughgoing analysis of the true facts only could lead to questions about where Henry had been at ten this morning, and how many times you saw Robert hit him last night, and why you didn't intervene a week ago Tuesday when Stanley took marbles from both of them. Say the least possible: rule of safety. Indeed, if you had to say things to grown-ups, say what they clearly intended to hear, what they had set up expectations for. Tell the truth, they pleaded, but what they meant was a truth for which they had braced themselves in advance.

The lady pulled at the strap of the evening dress. "So that's the truth, isn't it? On that night when your mother had the baby, Mrs. Cobden came over of her own accord. She made the offer. She heard all the noise and said she would stay."

Lorie nodded.

"You're sure now? I want to get it right."

"It's right." It might be right, anyhow—at one point or other, imagination had presented it with verisimilitude.

"So now we know exactly what happened." Triumph enhanced the visitor's looks; when she stood beaming in the doorway, you realized again how pretty she was. "You were a darling. I can't thank you enough."

"It was nothing." She lay on the bed after the visitor was gone. "Nothing" was not quite accurate; what it had been was a typical adult irrelevance. Whether a neighbor had been asked to babysit or had come of her own accord—what possible difference? Actually, the one event that stood out from that distant evening was her mother's search for her blue-striped blouse. "But I have to have it." Clutching the half-packed suitcase, her mother had stood in the maternity dress that could now be put away for next time. "Mom, just go, we'll find it." "I know, you'll forget." "No, honest." "I have to look decent, coming home from the hospital." Another irrelevance: each time she went off to have a baby, what worried her most was how she would look coming home with her rejuvenated figure. "Someplace around, we'll find it." It had, of course, been some place around. It had been—it still was—among the pile of improvised blankets which covered

Ellen's dolls. One of these days it would be found, there would be a crisis.

Indeed, that impending event was so clear that when she heard the screams from the next room, she thought, Starting already, Ellen's going to catch it. She lay back as the noise grew louder.

"Henry, did you take it? Answer me this minute."

Not the blouse after all—her mother would never sound so hysterical.

"Were you in there? Robert, were you?"

A frantic denial, interrupted by coughing—she must be shaking him.

"Prissy, what about—don't cry, I'm asking everyone else too. Prissy, stop crying for three seconds and tell us. Did you or didn't you?"

Prissy evidently had not. Stanley was next, then Ellen. A pause—she was on the way even before the summons was uttered. "Lorie? Get in here."

Definitely not a blouse, she realized as soon as she walked in: the look on her mother's face held pure alarm. It was one of the few times she was conscious of the size of the family as an encumbrance. Generally there was a feeling of confusion tempered by solidity—someone was always around to keep an eye. But now, standing in the doorway of her parents' bedroom, she knew surveillance could be inadequate. She looked at Prissy's streaked face, at Stanley's furtive movements as he tried to slip out of sight, and she had a sense of too many people, too much to handle, too many directions from which the unexpected could come. Even after she had found out what was missing—a bottle of sleeping pills from the top shelf of the bathroom medicine chest—even after she'd gotten it straight and issued a denial for herself, the uneasiness remained. There were times when authority couldn't cope, things could get out of hand.

Mary was called from her puzzle; for a minute things subsided, then fear took over again. "Where's Lance?"

"Don't be silly. Lance would never—"

"Would so. Remember last week he was acting so crazy—"

"Find Lance. Robert, Henry, Stanley, don't just stand there."

". . . saw him this morning."

"Six hours, dopey. He could be dead by now."

"How long till you die from sleeping pills?"

"Oh, God, if that child—"

"Chris, listen. Maybe you're mistaken, there weren't so many at all."

"Nineteen," her mother's hollow voice answered.

"You can't be—"

"I am sure. Twenty-five to start—Dr. Salmon told me. I took three that time my back hurt after the trip, and one when Ellen threw up, I had to get some sleep, and two for you that awful weekend when—"

"Okay, okay." From the look on her father's face, she knew it was not okay—sweat poured down from his bald skull.

"How long till you die from sleeping pills?"

"Maybe he took only half of them, then he'll—"

"How long till you die from sleeping pills?"

"Children! One more word out of you."

"If we'd call the police . . ." But though the police, it seemed, were not to be called, expeditions were dispatched: Robert to the playground, Stanley to the vacant field around the corner, Ellen to the lobby, Pris to the Mayhew Corner Store. Lorie herself, though ordered to check apartments 2S and 4H, in which there were children Lance's age, went to the nook between the fourth floor and the roof where someone needing quiet could hide out, and there she found him.

Then it started again.

"Lance, do you know how you worried us."

"I was right up there." He waved an indeterminate arm.

"Why anyone would want to sit on the stairs."

"Didn't you realize we'd be looking? Lance, answer me."

But he was an old hand at not answering—she saw the look come over his face which could be construed as sullenness but was simply part of his apparatus for withdrawal. He was the one child who, in the midst of all of them, could seclude himself, retire into privacy—questions bounced uselessly off.

"Four whole hours on a staircase when all the other children—"

". . . explain why you won't play with—"

"If you'd try to tell us, Lance."

And all the time, she could see that he knew about the pills. He had that look of secreting something, drawing himself around it. He always knew things. He was the only one who had seen them take Mr. Cobden's body down the hall, he had gone past the cordon of adults prepared one way or another to shield them, and now he could tell them about the pills if only they would stop asking the unanswerable questions about his attitude and pose the simple one about who did what.

Or must she pose it? "Lance, those pills that were in the bathroom—do you know who took them?"

"Yes."

"Well, who?" She could feel her parents' gaze on her head.

"Mrs. Cobden," his relieved voice said.

"My God, Lance, why didn't you tell us?"

Now they would kick this around. Why didn't he, and how could he, and try to explain? But eventually they laid off and the story emerged. Mrs. Cobden took them when she came over this afternoon. No, he didn't actually see her take them, but he saw her go into the bathroom and then come out five minutes later. It was when she came over to borrow the thermos because she was going on a boat ride. She was terribly excited. A boat ride on such a beautiful night—she would wear her yellow dress to match the thermos.

A dress to match their thermos—it gave the unmistakable touch of reality. Sideways, Lance's lips delivered the words, and with them the story came alive. You saw Mrs. Cobden's hands fluttering at the little barrettes. You saw her offering more effusive thanks than a beat-up thermos really deserved. You saw her indifferent gaze pass over whichever child happened to be in her way. And you also saw her—you were able to imagine her—snooping in someone else's medicine cabinet, reaching down from the top shelf the bottle that no one else would dream of touching.

Two of the boys moved restively—they had been cooped up a long time.

"All right, kids—that's that."

But it wasn't quite—who would suppose it could be? When the two babies had finally been put to sleep, and Robert and Henry separated from the final bout of the day, and the prepared-mix brownies taken, too late, from the oven where someone was supposed to have been watching them—in the lull that followed, she heard her parents.

"Just don't understand you, Christine. In a place with nine children, to leave sleeping pills out where—"

"Stan, it wasn't the children."

"Every law of safety. Every precept of common sense."

"Stan, the children *did not take them.*"

"Typical of the way you pay attention to little things, and the big ones that mean safety—"

"So I ignore the big things." There was a dangerous note in her mother's voice. One of them had better laughingly retract pretty soon.

"No sense of proportion at all." Anger would flare up on her father's face, which was really a youthful one. Seeing him at his rare moments of composure, with his bald head, his gentle look, people thought, Just right for someone with nine children. But he was bald when he was twenty; before he had even one child, he was that fellow who'd lost all his hair; when perspiration dripped from the shiny skull and emotion played under it, you realized how young he was for the big family he had produced. ". . . hysterical if someone's three minutes late from the playground, and you run half a mile to give some child a sweater, but in a matter of life and death—"

"Okay, I'm a terrible mother. I hate my children. I want them poisoned with sleeping pills." Her mother's voice was wildly self-pitying, her father's coldly harsh. Too late for any light retractions now—soon her mother would say, If you had any consideration for what I've been through, and her father would answer, You wanted all these goddamn children, and a whole evening of gloom would go by before that reconciliation which by its sticky nature and public show of affection proved itself equally boring.

". . . something happens, be all your fault."

"What can happen? Every child is perfectly—"

"To Doreen Cobden."

Silence. Her mother, wearing the injured look, must be glaring out the window. "What's going to happen to her?" she said at last.

"If she takes an overdose of your sleeping medicine."

"She's had her own medicine for weeks. Her doctor gave it to her after the burn."

"Then why would she take yours?"

"I suppose she ran out of her own, and when she couldn't reach her doctor, he was away for the weekend—"

"Yes. Exactly what you would suppose."

"Just what do you mean by that?"

"A poor little woman without a husband, struggling to get by on no money at all."

Her mother's voice was distant—she must have turned away. "The poor struggling little woman was at the movies from two till six Thursday afternoon. Double feature."

"You don't think she's entitled to some pleasure?"

"Know when the last time I was able to—"

"You'd like to be her, I suppose. Someone without children."

"Maybe she didn't want them."

"You know she did—she told us. She was longing for them. She couldn't have any because of some accident."

A crash: riding around the living-room rug on his tricycle, Stanley must have pulled down the curtains. Neither of them moved; this fight was more important even than curtains. "You're so sorry for her. If you'd show a little consideration for what I've been through."

"You wanted all these goddamn children."

"I didn't want them if my husband wasn't going to be

decent." Her mother was crying; simultaneously, she would look over her shoulder to see if the tears were having effect. But it was much too early for that; even she, Lorie, understood the timing.

"Plucky little woman like that, we ought to be helping her more."

"Why doesn't she help herself?"

"She did. Look at that business she started. The shopping and baking and delivering—someone all alone in her own kitchen."

"If she's so wonderful, why doesn't she go on with it?"

"She wishes she could. But there's some injury from the burn, she was explaining to me the other day."

"I see."

"I met her in the elevator," he said coldly. "This tendon on her arm was injured by the burn. Even though the skin is healed, it might be permanently injured unless she's careful. No heavy lifting—the doctor was definite."

"Well, she's lifting herself right now into a motorboat. Tendon and all. With a yellow dress and our yellow thermos —so cute. I mean, you're so sorry for her, and there she is in a motorboat."

"You hate motorboats, you always say so. Last time I suggested that we rent one—"

"Oh, my God, you really are—"

She couldn't hear what her mother thought her father really was, because new crashes sounded from the living room, and when this had been settled, or maybe the curtain was down for good, they were back on the sleeping pills again.

". . . nineteen of them, you're sure?"

"I told you." Her mother by now sounded sullen—this was longer than their fights usually went on.

"Plus what she had—"

"Why would she take mine if she had any of her own?"

"I'm not saying she did. She might. All that trouble folding in on her, and the example set by her husband—we ought to be prepared."

"You going out to buy a stomach pump?" Her mother was always sarcastic when she was close to tears.

"I'm certainly going to be around when she comes back from that boat."

"Around where?"

"In her apartment. Waiting to talk to her."

"Fine. I can do all the dishes by myself, and Ellen can wait till next weekend for that shelf, and Stanley, well, suppose you don't fix his bike pedal like you promised."

"Christine, listen. Those pills—it ever occur to you she might have them with her this minute?"

"Mixed with lemonade in our thermos?"

"Go on, laugh. But if a perilously distraught woman is in trouble . . ."

"Seven hundred boats on the Sound. What kind of trouble can someone get into?"

"Seven thousand boats, and an accident could happen. I just hope she makes it back to her apartment, that's all."

"Where you'll be waiting for her."

"Yes. Where I'll be waiting. And if you weren't so self-centered, so wrapped up in your little problems."

That finished it, of course. Conceivably her mother might have come around to sharing his anxiety, for a second there had been sympathy in her voice. Now she would look at the unwashed dishes, the piles of diapers, the cranky children. Little problems. Little problems. . . . Another two hours, at least, added to the fight.

She moved away from the door. Was her father right? Was there really danger? For a second as he said "perilously distraught," she had felt a sense of something ominous; Mrs. Cobden had been raised to the dimensions of one who could make dire things happen.

Then she sat on her own bed, she saw again the woman in her scoop-neck dresses. All this fuss for someone so silly. First that man coming with his intense eyes, and then the lady in her black evening dress, and now her parents ruining a perfectly good night. The fact was, Mrs. Cobden wasn't worth it. Even the speculation about her could be handled by simple logic. Could she have children, for example—anyone with half an eye could tell that it didn't matter whether she could have them or not, because children were the last thing that interested her. If all of them came into the lobby at the same time, Mrs. Cobden wouldn't notice them. Mary could put on her most beatific smile, and Stanley could do his gorilla act, and she, Lorie, could be wearing her new blue checked dress, and Mrs. Cobden's gaze would go over them, past them, as if they were of no more concern than the plastic plants set in colored stones in the corner. In fact, the only time she knew they were alive was when their father happened to come in with them, and then she practically fell over herself cooing, twitching all of them under the chin, saying if this wasn't the most adorable baby, she just loved babies.

But for some reason, simple logic was failing them tonight. There was something wrong; sitting right here on this bed, even she, Lorie, had made statements that were not true— at least half of which, now she thought about it, could not be true. What was going on? What was there about Mrs. Cobden that could get all of them so upset?

21

There was nothing to be upset about, Jane thought. She had found out definitely how Doreen killed her husband; she had confirmed this premeditated act through talking to the child who was present when the premeditation was going on, but still there was nothing upsetting. Or, rather, nothing that meant any danger to Tony. Though he was out with Doreen in a boat, the idea was distasteful but not alarming—whoever heard of an accident in a motorboat? The worst that could happen was what she had imagined earlier: his eating Doreen's unappetizing food, sipping her notion of an appropriate drink. Along with the tuna-fish sandwiches, there would be . . . well, some mixture of pineapple juice and lemonade. Yes: just the sort of concoction Doreen would consider suitably gay. She would unscrew the top of a thermos and hold it out with her coy little smile—didn't he like it? she would ask.

He wouldn't like it, but he would force it down anyhow. That was Tony. Amiable. Sweet. Yes, Doreen, delicious, he would say. Which gave her a second reason for not being upset: no one could possibly have anything against Tony. Even a woman who had killed her own husband, or at least had planned to be out of the kitchen at a time when he would find a lethal drink in it—even that kind of woman would not want to harm Tony Bassett. Why should she? For a month he had taken care of her, done her favors—she wouldn't be harboring any secret grudges against him, and she wouldn't be hatching any dangerous plans either as the two of them rode with hundreds of other small craft through the still waters of Staunton harbor.

In fact, waiting here at the Staunton dock, she, Jane, was doing exactly the right thing. Almost eight o'clock. Even if they cruised awhile, slowed down for that pineapple-lemon drink, a motorboat ride could be extended just so long; sooner or later they would pull into one of those vacant moorings down below. For all she knew, one of the three men standing there now was the boat's prospective buyer: that one with the sneakers and the dark sweat shirt, or the one with two children hanging onto his arm, or even the elderly one, with his feet dangling over the edge. He was reading a book, but he didn't look as if he wanted to wait forever. Very soon, then. Say ten minutes. Ten minutes during which she had to stand right here, not budge. They all could look askance at her—someone in a long black evening dress on a dock—but it didn't matter. Let those three girls snicker as they regarded her, and the two men drinking Cokes give her a funny look—she had to be here when they docked.

She had to be here because Tony would understand right away. She looked over at the gangplank, where a young boy in dungarees and tee shirt walked lightly up the resilient boards, and superimposed on his figure was Tony's. Tony understanding that his wife adored him. Tony making some excuse to Doreen. Tony managing to get off with her for a second so immediately, in the midst of this public place, they could establish the fact of their privacy.

But first, of course, he had to come. She was starved; nothing to eat except Mrs. Merimee's coffee since noon. She could smell hot dogs from the stand at the edge of the beach, but if she walked over, there would be a stretch where for a few yards the boat house cut off her view of the dock, and she might miss them. Especially now that it was getting dark, she might miss them. Darkness seemed to come more precipitately here by the water—the orange glow that had been in the sky a few minutes ago was gone. The boats were blurring too—she could no longer make out the small swaying shapes that had been at the neck of the harbor, and that hope had ascribed to Tony.

Once it was dark, they must come, mustn't they? When she went into the boat house, she stood near the door, so she could keep watch on that gangplank up which the returning boaters must walk. "When do you close?"

The fellow looked up from his paper. "Ten, fifteen minutes. Soon as I get finished."

"Then all the boats have to be in within fifteen minutes?"

"What's that?"

"Then all the boats have to be in within fifteen minutes," her brightly defensive voice repeated.

"Why should they?"

"Well, if you're closing . . . If . . ." Far down along the dock, a boat slid into a mooring, two figures detached themselves. That taller one, still hunched over, reaching out a hand? . . . "Tony. Tony." A strange face peered up from under a cap.

"They can stay out till midnight. All night. Why not?" he said.

"I thought there must be some specified time."

"You looking for someone?" His glance, abstracted until now, settled on her dress, made a judgment about it, translated this into imperfectly concealed amazement.

"My husband."

"He alone?"

"Could I hire a boat?" she unexpectedly heard herself answer.

"Where would you look for him?"

She waited while a family came in, piled bundles of no recognizable shape into a locker too small for them. "They're coming from right over there. Stoneycrest."

"You know how many ways to get from Stoneycrest? Out toward Rawley, where the Sound gets wider. Or heading south, past Heather Point. On this beautiful night, not a breeze blowing, what's to stop them from pulling up at one of those little coves, getting out of the—lady, don't look like that. Didn't mean to upset you—husbands do that all the time."

No. Husbands do that only if they feel injured. If they

think their wife has treated them shabbily, they have reason
for anger and resentment.

Or didn't he have reason? Was it only in her deluded mind
that he thought she was out with Alan? There was a phone
booth against the wall, she held her silly evening bag with
one hand while with the other she fished for change.

"Sheila? It's Mrs. Bassett. How's everything?"

Everything was fine, the cheerful voice told her. Lovely.
She shouldn't worry a bit. Betsy didn't eat all her vegetables,
but she loved the custard. "That orange flavor. You said
only half a jar, but—"

"Sheila, listen. When Mr. Bassett came home, did he notice
the dress?"

Another family trooped in. "How can I open the locker?"
a boy was yelling. "How can I open—"

"What? I didn't understand."

"I said, when she liked that custard so much—"

"Mr. Bassett, Sheila. That's what I'm asking."

"I did try it," the boy shouted. "Right two times past
twenty-four, then left to eighteen—"

"Sheila, talk louder. Mr. Bassett came home, and then what'd
you say?"

". . . meet you? Didn't he?" The girl's round face would
be dismayed; she would straighten the telephone wire, which
sometimes got tangled with the overgrown philodendron hanging from an upper shelf of the divider. In her experience,
husbands and wives—especially husbands and wives in the
teacher category—made neatly coordinated plans, allotted
every precious minute during which a sitter was paid for,
went out on meticulously prearranged schedules.

"Arrangements a little mixed up. And I thought, if he didn't
know about the evening dress," she said laughingly.

"Not left, dummy. Right. Right two times past thirty-one."

"Mixed up," she repeated, above still another importunate
voice. "So I wondered. Exactly what happened when he
came—oh, please don't make so much noise."

Sheila's voice grew perversely softer—or was it just the

sounds from the clanging lock that made it appear so? Mr. Bassett had come home around noon—was that what the reticent adolescent voice was saying? And of course he saw the dress. How could he not? Hanging right there on the door, after all, with all those pins . . . A pause, baffled, apprehensive. This not only defied experience, but undermined it. Didn't they? . . . Wouldn't he? . . . Wasn't she? . . .

"Of course, Sheila, of course. He'll be here any second. Just a little late, I guess, sometimes things mixed up." "I told you right past thirty-one," the boy was shouting as she hung up.

Of course, any second. Just because the view of a dress must have been compounded in Tony's mind with the threat implicit in his wife's unguarded talk, just because he had fallen into logical but, as it turned out, false assumptions about what she was doing tonight . . . just because of those mistakes, he would not stay out in a motorboat with Doreen. In fact, the prospective buyer still was waiting—the one with the dark sweat shirt. The other two were gone, so this must be the man. He looked not simply like one waiting to conclude a sale, but one who would have set a definite time for it—ten more minutes and they must be here. The only reason they were not here yet was that Doreen wanted to see the reflection of the moon on water. You're so wonderful the way you know exactly how to steer, she would say. Tony would be looking at his watch this second, trying to make better time.

"I beg your pardon."

"Yes?"

"I noticed you waiting—that is, were you planning to buy a boat?"

A pause, while her bare shoulders, her long skirt went under scrutiny. "You have one to sell?" he asked.

"Not exactly. I'm just—"

"What kind of boat?"

She took a step backward.

"I might be interested. Girlie," he added after another close inspection.

"I thought you were someone else," Jane said.

"Tell me what's to sell, maybe we can do business. Nice boat? Pretty? Or maybe not a boat at all—"

"Oh, never mind." Even walking away with dignity was not possible; these planks weren't made for high-heeled shoes, when she stumbled she heard his laughter. She stood on the grassy bank. She had missed them, that was all. That man was not the buyer, but someone else had been, the transaction had already taken place, and despite her watchfulness she had missed them. There were plenty of times it could have happened: when she stepped into the drugstore to call a taxi, or when she got off at the beach entrance instead of here at the dock, or even during those fifteen minutes in the taxi. The new image superseded all old ones: she and Tony within a few unseeing yards of each other as they drove in different directions on the road between Stoneycrest and Staunton. In which case, Tony would be . . . not home, he would definitely not go home. He would have taken Doreen to her apartment, and been unable to break away. You're so wonderful to check my bank books look over my insurance help move my dishes . . . against the familiar cloying demands he would not be able to muster the usual defenses; tonight he would be stuck.

Another phone call, then. Another taxi. Another walk past the plastic plants in the lobby. She heard noises from across the hall as she rang—Henry and Robert still fighting? Prissy still crying? She also heard footsteps behind Doreen's door. They reminded her how unprepared she was. I just wanted to make sure my husband was all right—at another woman's apartment, any remark would be inappropriate, any move would be handing Doreen another triumph.

"Yes?" A man with a bald head opened the door.

"Is Mrs. Cobden here?"

"I'm waiting for her myself." Under that smooth forehead, his eyes widened; once more, in the shock of someone else's look, she was reading the transcript of her own grotesque appearance.

"Please excuse my dress—I just came from a party." The gratuitous fib hung for a second in the hallway—the man received it without interest. He wasn't, in fact, interested in her; he was reluctant to have her come in, but she came anyhow, edging past him into the gaudy confusion of Doreen's living room. Colors and shapes crowded in on her—little knick-knacks, Tony had said after his first visit here, but he had understated as usual, nothing had suggested the profusion of design, the swirling prints, the objects that filled every inch of shelf or table.

"Are you a friend of Doreen's?" she asked.

"Her neighbor. From across the hall."

"Then you're the one with all those children." He was also she realized, much younger than she had thought. The bald head was deceptive—under it the features were suitable for one who would hoist a wailing child on his shoulders, give piggyback rides, show a boy how to hold a bat. But why wasn't he busy with all that now? At nine o'clock on a Saturday night, what was he doing in Doreen's apartment?

"Such darling children. I know the oldest. Lorie. That is, I was talking to her just awhile ago."

He nodded, uncurious about why she had talked to Lorie, unwilling even to respond to pleasantries about his own children. He isn't seeing me, she thought. He's wholly involved in something else.

"Do you expect them . . . Doreen . . . soon?"

"I hope so." From that bald head, the most perfunctory nod.

"I certainly hope so too." Her little laugh accomplished nothing: no friendliness in him, no comfort in her. "Do you know where she is?"

"She's out in a motorboat."

Yes. With my husband. The two of them going the long way around past Rawley, or heading south at Heather Point, or maybe, nice night like this, stopping at one of those little coves. . . . Was there any point telling him? Would it advance anything?

"You a friend of hers?" He turned suddenly, his tight look went over her.

"I know her from the high school. My husband teaches there." She spoke with careful ambiguity, conscious anew of the anomaly of her looks. "I guess I should introduce myself. I'm Jane Bassett. My husband is Tony Bassett."

"You a good friend of Mrs. Cobden's?"

His tone was not in the least casual; what it meant, what it plainly was intended to mean, was, Did she like Mrs. Cobden? Which answer was the tactical one? Which would get him to talk? She looked at his strained face, and she was more than ever convinced he had something he might talk about if properly approached. This was not just a neighborly visit—it couldn't be. She studied the spot on the coffee table between a dresden shepherdess and a fluted vase. Yes, I like Doreen. No, I don't like Doreen. Which one? She had defended Doreen to Mrs. Merimee, sung her praises in falsely glowing terms, and the result was catastrophic, it had almost closed off all communication. This man also looked sensitive, somber.

"You can't really be a good friend of hers." Breathless, she took the plunge. "I mean, this apartment. All this clutter. Someone who would go in for this kind of stuff."

Wrong answer: she could see right away. His face had frozen.

"Oh, I don't mean she isn't sweet. Darling. Such an easy-going disposition." Won't do you any good. You ruined it. Whatever it is that's keeping him here with that taut alertness, he'll never tell you now.

She sat in a chair covered in a paisley print. "Does Doreen know you're coming?"

"No."

"You mean, she doesn't expect you at all?"

"That's right."

"You're just—waiting? Whenever she comes in?"

"Yes."

"It must be important." Again that falsely jocular smile. "After all, a Saturday night, dozens of other things you probably want to do."

His gaze, stiff with resentment, went over her, and she
thought, he'll never tell me now. The longer I stay, the less
chance of my finding anything out. Besides, why should she
stay: she had pictured Doreen as having only Tony to hold
onto, clinging to him, but here was someone else obviously
making himself available. In any logical appraisal, this man
with his stubborn presence ought to diminish her concern.

She would go home, then—why had she waited this long?
Ten minutes to walk home, and five to listen to Sheila's report
about what Betsy did or did not eat, and another twenty
minutes to change and clean up the apartment, because despite her best efforts Sheila could never remember which pot
went where, and by the time she had finished all that, Tony
would surely—

"Prissy's sick. She's crying." It was Lorie's mother standing
in the doorway. But how different she looked from this afternoon, and what a belligerent tone she took toward her husband.

"This is Mrs.—uh—Bassett." When the man turned, light
filtered through Doreen's pink lampshade onto his bald head.

"We met this afternoon." The nod from those red-rimmed
eyes was not a friendly one—Jane was perforce included in
any stance she took against her husband. "Prissy's crying," she
repeated.

"That's too bad."

"She expected you to read to her, you promised." The
woman had a toneless voice, and Jane recognized it right
away. Any wife would recognize it—any wife who had also
fought with her husband, worked herself into a conviction of
his awfulness, resolved not to let tears weaken her rage.

"She's hysterical, practically," the woman who had Lorie's
high forehead and wide mouth went accusingly on. "She'll
get sick."

"I thought you said she was sick already."

Her heart went out to the woman. Didn't she know that in
fighting with husbands, you had to be accurate above all else?
Husbands tore into inaccuracies, hung onto them with fierce

righteousness. The main thread of your argument might be—definitely was—impeccable, but the men went looking for some small irrelevancy, inflated it out of all proportion, displayed it as though their virtue was thereby vindicated and their case thus proved.

"Stanley's knee is bleeding, and Lance is God knows where, and Mary . . . I mean, with nine children needing you, you're just going to stand at that window?"

"What it looks like." In fact, he turned again toward the window, so he didn't have his back to his wife, but he wasn't quite facing her either.

"I'm supposed to do everything. All the work."

Silence. No, not complete silence. She herself couldn't control a small cough. It interrupted the feud for an instant, but only an instant.

"Doreen might not walk in here till late, you ever think of that?"

Another shrug; his hand rubbed along the shade, to which was attached a row of tufted green balls.

"She wasn't going out on that motorboat alone. She has someone with her."

My husband is with her—again the words quivered on her lips. She said nothing; no point in saying anything. By fighting in her presence, they made it clear they wanted to ignore her, they were in a state to do nothing but ignore her.

"When Doreen finally does come"—Lorie's mother brushed the hair off her face—"she might not be so anxious for any cozy talk with a neighbor."

"You're absolutely right." His voice was icy too.

"But you're so sure of yourself, of course. Your great powers of persuasion."

What was it he had to persuade Doreen? To accept money? To move to another apartment? To have dinner with them a week from tomorrow? She opened her mouth again, realized her words could only fall into the void that had been established so neither of them could hear the other. Darling, please come home and make love to me . . . the woman could say something as forthright as that, and it wouldn't penetrate. In fact, she was saying it; what else did she mean when she raved on about Stanley or Lance or Pris?

". . . tell them, then. Your own children, but you can't be bothered with them."

"I'll see the kids in the morning."

"They'll just have to understand. Mrs. Cobden counts more than they do with their father."

"In the morning," the man said—simultaneously, his shoulders sagged, and sympathy, illogic as usual, swung to him. He can't help it, she wanted to explain to this woman standing here distraught and furious. You're absolutely right, and he ought to go home with you this minute, but he really feels he has a mission here. That's what Doreen does to them—ties them in knots, makes them want to protect her.

Jane leaned back. How they loved each other, she contentedly thought. And how skillfully each had practiced to make the other miserable. Without thinking, she could deliver the rest of this woman's tirade; she knew every wild accusation, every passionate hyperbole, every sarcastic insult designed to cover wounded pride. She could deliver the tirade, of course, because she had delivered it already—it or its equivalent. This morning, and the day before, and two days before that, while Tony stood in just the position this man was in.

Though only the back of that smooth head was visible, she also knew what emotions were on his face. Anger. Doubt. Irresolution. Pride. . . . all the emotions Tony would wear. This man did not in the least resemble Tony—he was shorter and at least ten years older, and his baldness gave him a wholly different aspect—but by being in Tony's role, he once again evoked Tony. It was Tony over there next to the fringed window shade. While he stood indecisive, Tony would rub his hand across his face, mess up those bushy eyebrows—she would have to wet the tip of her finger and flatten them. What gesture did this woman have—something which connoted intimacy and yet looked in public like any proper wifely act?

". . . in that yellow dress to match our thermos. Just adorable."

"Christine, shut up about that thermos."

"Suppose something does happen?"

"Can't you ever be serious?"

Serious about what?—something extraneous had entered the conversation, altered it. "Is anything wrong?" That was her own voice, asking the thin question.

They both turned to her, but not in amity. The pause lenghtened—she could sense the animus both of them felt for each other being transferred, unfairly but inevitably, to her. Then the man shook his head. "Nothing at all."

"I really—"

"Nothing."

Should she press it? Should she ask again what it was about that thermos that had them so upset? Hating each other—believing for a few hours they hated each other—they could hardly relish talking to a third person, and why should they? A yellow thermos . . . something about a yellow thermos . . . Doreen had probably borrowed it once before and returned it with the dregs of her sticky drink not thoroughly washed out. Or it had been promised for the day to the people in 2F, they had asked for it first. Any trivial explanation was likely because at a time like this any trivia could heighten a fight, inflame it.

Besides, the fight was moving on. ". . . can't swim, did you know that? Another of the things no one ever taught her." A hopeless tone had come into the woman's voice; she must know she wouldn't win, no matter what she said he would wait here for Doreen. "Your plucky Mrs. Cobden can't drive a car, and she can't get those heavy platters down from a shelf, and some big strong neighbor has to come in if that light bulb gets stuck. Only now it turns out she can't swim either. She told me this afternoon. So you could be the one.

You could play teacher," her bitter voice flung at his intractable back.

No answer. What answer was there?

". . . started to drown, if she started to do that, she might pull you down too. It happens. Those people in a motorboat last April—remember?"

"No, I don't."

"This couple. He'd been diving champion. East Coast Intercollegiate Champion. Only she couldn't swim a stroke— the marks of her fingers were on his neck when they found him. So if you're really worried, why don't you go down to the Sound this minute. Go on. Be a sucker. Do it right."

The man by the window who was not Tony and yet evoked Tony made a gesture of distaste. Such nonsense. Such fantasy. He waved a contemptuous hand and turned his bald head on both of them. He did not in the least evoke Tony—that comfort was gone. Tony was out on that water, in a boat with someone who couldn't swim.

She was conscious of Lorie's mother calling her as she left, and for a second she was tempted to stop, explain that it was all right, not their unceremonious manners at all making her leave. But how could you explain to someone who was furious at her husband that she was really the lucky one? Her husband, at least, was here. Dry. Safe. Accessible. It was someone else's husband, this evening, who had pre-empted the role of sucker.

22

"But I thought the Coast Guard was supposed to save people."
She gripped the telephone.

"Right, miss. Anyone in danger."

"This is danger, I told you." Whoever had held this phone before had been eating something greasy—her fingerprints left swirls on the black plastic. "A woman in a boat . . . a woman who killed someone . . ."

"Who'd she kill again?" the conversational voice asked at the other end.

"Her husband. I already—"

"You tell the police about all this?" From his easygoing tone, she tried to visualize him. He was leaning back at his desk. He was chewing the end of a pencil. He was sending a quietly amused glance to someone across the room.

"It just happed this afternoon. I mean, I just found out."

"Possible murder—something for the police, wouldn't you think?"

"Line up for three-legged race," blared the loudspeaker outside the phone booth. "Last call for three-legged race."

"It's an emergency. They're in a motorboat."

"I'm afraid you want another department, Miss, this is the—"

"Oh, please don't hang up. I waited twenty minutes to get you. I had three other departments already."

"Line up now for three-legged race!"

Her hand slid along the greasy earpiece. "If you would just give me advice. Tell me how to go about—"

"We can't do anything about murder, Miss." He pronounced

"murder" with a slight hesitation before it; that amused glance he was sending across the room turned briefly into a wink.

"My husband's out there with her. In a motorboat."

"You said it was her husband she killed. She has nothing against your husband, does she?"

There it was again: the nagging idea. What had Tony been trying to tell her, these past two days? What rifts between him and Doreen had he hinted at during that acrimonious session this morning when she was feeling too bemused or too injured or too self-centered to listen?

"They're getting on fine, aren't they? This lady and your husband?"

"You have it all wrong."

"Okay, Miss, don't get sore." Another of the derisive pauses. ". . . kind of boat?"

"What?"

"I said, what kind of motorboat?"

Did it mean he was planning to help her after all? Or was this part of his idea of fun, stringing along someone who sounded hysterical on a quiet Saturday night? "I don't know—a small one. Very small motorboat."

"And their projected route?"

She didn't even know definitely they were still on the water. Tony's schedule had seemed breathtakingly obvious to her when she left Doreen's apartment. He would have driven to the Stoneycrest dock, taken the boat with Doreen to Staunton where the prospective buyer was waiting, come back to Stoneycrest for the car. No need for this aimless running around— all she had to do was check the parking lot, see if his car was still here. Sensible. Simple.

But in her mind had been the Stoneycrest parking lot as it was three hundred and sixty-four nights a year: a pretty apron of concrete with lindens between it and the baseball field on the left, a church steeple rising on the hill behind the boat house, an all-but-invisible, hand-painted sign pointing the way to the boats because if you came here at all it was assumed you didn't need signs, you knew your way around. There were signs tonight: FIREMEN'S CARNIVAL, they said, under the streams of colored bunting. Signs, bands, roller coasters, tents . . . from the phone booth she looked out at the blazing disorder. "Three-year-old girl lost," the loudspeaker shouted. "Blonde, wearing a red sunsuit, says her name is Barbie."

Wandering through the confusion of lights and people, had Barbie's parents also laughed off panic, and little by little acknowledged its power, and finally felt it deepen beyond the power of logic or reason?

At the other end of this phone, the man was waiting. "Must you have their exact route before you look for them?"

"A description also, of course."

"She's wearing a yellow dress," she said. "To match the— I mean, yellow." Doreen and the yellow dress and the yellow thermos—what had troubled Lorie's parents about this catalogue? What small fact would set things moving, if she knew how to find it? The loudspeaker was thunderous—she could hardly think.

"What about your husband? What's he wearing?"

"I don't exactly know." How could I know?—I haven't seen him since nine this morning.

"I'm afraid you have the wrong department, miss."

"Then why'd you ask me all these questions? Was it just to bait me? Did you know perfectly well the whole time you had no intention of—"

He had hung up, of course. When she wandered outside, the noise was louder. Barbie must have been found, no more mention of her, but fireworks would be starting, said the tireless voice. Best seats for fireworks on jetty rocks. Go now to jetty rocks for best seats for fireworks. At one end of the dock, a man in uniform was standing. "How do you know if there's an accident?" she said.

"Never an accident. That roller coaster looks tippy, but you don't have to be afraid, it never yet—"

"I mean, on the water."

"Never an accident on the water."

"There was in April. That couple."

"What couple?"

"He was a diving champion. East Coast Collegiate Champion."

"Two boys lost for a while one weekday. A Tuesday. The reason I remember Tuesday is that—"

"She couldn't swim at all. She must have been clinging to him. There were marks on his neck."

"What was his name?"

"I don't know."

"How did the boat tip over?"

"I don't know that either."

"If you don't know, how can anyone help you?"

When he moved into the light, what had seemed like a uniform dissolved into an old brimmed cap, a jacket with obscure insignia—what authority did he have anyhow? She stared at the water while the last call for the potato-sack race went out into the receptive night. "Look at that lady," a child's voice said piercingly across the field, and after a second she realized she was the lady. Standing in a long black evening dress at a firemen's carnival, she offered an enjoyable target for sport. She was a discordant note, but she didn't spoil anything, quite the contrary—her odd looks simply emphasized the wholesome jollity available to everyone else.

She was dressed wrong and she was in the wrong place too—no reason for Tony, having delivered a boat, to come back to the place where boats were tied. If he had gone through with his plans, if he and Doreen were off that limitless expanse of water, he would simply get his car and leave. She looked again at the parking lot, splashed with shadows from the tippy but fully accredited roller coaster. Blue-and-red lights festooned for the occasion shone on the license plates, but she didn't know her license. A college graduate, the smartest girl in the Eco Department, and she had never bothered to learn the numbers that distinguished their tan sedan from every other tan sedan in a suburban parking lot. All she knew was the name of the overdue library book in the glove compartment and the color of Betsy's outgrown sweater which had been rolled up for three weeks on the floor. Suppose she ran between those tangled lines, an oddball in high-heeled shoes and evening dress, opening every glove compartment. It all would start again: You don't even know the license number of your own car, miss? Well, how can we help you if you don't even know . . .

"Janey, stop crying."

She couldn't stop.

"Nothing to cry about, is there?"

"I don't know our license number."

"Well, I know it, so why do you have to?" his reasonable voice said.

"Suppose you're lost, I can't even—"

"I'm not lost, I'm right here. If you'd stop crying you could—"

"Tony, I thought you were out in the boat."

"I was, but now I'm here."

"You and Doreen, only she can't swim, and that poor boy, after winning the diving championship . . ."

"What about him?"

"To be found with those marks on his neck."

"What's his name?"

Now Tony was asking her questions too. He was wearing his blue jersey, his tan pants. Of course—what else would he wear to go out in a boat except one of his two decent sport shirts, his only pair of non-school pants? A little logic—all that had been needed the whole time. "Where's Doreen?"

"I went out alone. . . . Jane, if you keep rubbing your eyes—there. That's better, isn't it?"

"Judging of the prettiest child contest is now being held in front of the bandstand. Judging of the prettiest child contest . . ."

"Why'd you go out alone?" she began again, but that familiar thoughtful look on his face meant not that the loudspeaker had interrupted him but that he was concentrating, taking his time.

"I was asking her too many questions. Questions about her and Martin. Doreen doesn't like that. If you ask her questions, you're cruel, heartless, sadistic. That's what she says—anything to avoid giving a straight answer."

When she moved, she saw that her dress was torn almost to the knee. Not the seam but the material—the dress was finished.

"You don't go out in a boat with someone who thinks you're a sadist—that's carrying things too far. But there was a business proposition—someone waiting at Staunton to pick up the boat." He sighed: one who had respect for business propositions even if they didn't happen to fit in with his plans. "So I took the boat over there and got the money and caught the nine-forty bus back here to get the car."

There: what she had figured. At least, almost what she had figured—there was a crucial difference. "What kind of questions did you ask her?"

"Jane, you okay now? You sure? Well, listen—I have to tell you something."

Below them, on the dock, a family must be coming in from their outing—she could hear the commands about holding tight, watching out, making sure Annie didn't fall in the water.

"Thing is, we've been all wrong. Anyhow, I've been wrong. Thinking that Martin committed suicide, accepting it. Because the truth is—"

"Tony, I know."

His hand, white, deprecatory, waved between her and the encircling darkness. "Oh, you guessed something, I realize—for weeks and weeks you've been telling me, and I wouldn't listen. But this is different. Not just guesswork at all. I found out specific facts."

"Facts?"

"About Martin. Or, rather, about Doreen. About what she did." When the clouds parted, moonlight shone on his intent eyes, his bushy eyebrows. "Jane, Martin didn't commit suicide. Doreen just made it look as if he did."

A tremendous excitement seized her. It had seemed like the most fortuitous of chances which had sent her, Jane, to collect money from the one person who knew the real story, but here was Tony having found it out too. It was symbolic; at the least, it was a testament to the closeness which had existed, which must have existed, during all the time when they had seemed so estranged. Because how else account for the wonder: that by going their separate ways, keeping to their wholly different courses, she and Tony had arrived at the same momentous discovery?

"Tony, darling, I know too."

"You mean . . . about her and Martin?" He waited while a boy in sneakers came up, padded silently past them. "Not just a guess? You know about that so-called suicide?"

"I know what really happened. I found out exactly how she—"

But his hand was on her mouth. It was the first time he had touched her intimately since they met. He had put an arm around her, wiped her eyes with his handkerchief, held her under the elbow when she stumbled, but these were gestures a man would make for any girl he met crying in the dark. But his fingers tremulous across her lips, that light but still insistent touch. . . . He's back with me, she thought. His hand tastes of salt water. His lips will taste salty too.

"Jane, must we talk about it?"

"But there's so much. The lies she told. The drawn-out tricks. Even that letter—that letter Martin wrote telling her to go back to Vermont, and she twisted it, made believe—"

"You and I know the truth. Isn't that all that matters?"

"But all those people thinking the wrong things . . . everyone who ever knew him—"

"Not quite everyone. Besides, we can't get Martin back—all we can do is injure someone else."

It was like Tony: even at this point, to think first of Mrs. Merimee and her son, want to protect them. At the same time, the question rose again: How did he find out? How did the extraordinary coincidence happen that had him able to penetrate in the same way that she did through Doreen's fabrications to the simple truth?

"I still don't understand. For you to get on to—"

"Jane, we've been obsessed by Doreen. For weeks we've thought about nothing else. Tonight can't we forget her? Put her out of our minds?"

She'll always be in some corner of my mind. Doreen saying coyly, You're so good to me. Doreen reaching inept fingers toward the butterfly barrettes. Doreen pouring cyanide into a glass on the kitchen table.

"If we start talking about her now . . ." Only the pressure of his hand on her arm indicated how he felt about the alternatives to talking.

And he was right, of course. After all the past grim weeks, tonight must be free from analysis of Doreen. They were standing triumphant now, exultant with the sense of their joint knowledge—two people for whom the fact of their discovering the truth about someone else was somehow linked with their rediscovering their love for each other.

But tomorrow they would talk about Doreen. Talk and talk and talk—they would go over every crafty maneuver, every diabolical move. In fact, she thought suddenly, it was just possible their certainty might falter. That iron-clad discovery about which both of them were so proud—as Mrs. Merimee had pointed out, there was no proof. You could never be entirely sure. There might never be a way to be sure.

Did that mean their love was going to falter too? At this moment it seemed entirely strong. Unassailable. But the past mistakes had been memorable ones; though you closed the door on them, pushed them out of sight, was there any real change in the circumstances that had given rise to them? Maybe the best you could hope was that they would peer out only occasionally to taunt you with the sense of your foolishness and the reminder of your frailty.

She gave a little shiver—wasn't there anything about which you could be wholly, radiantly clear? Must you always be conscious of the margin for doubt? "Janey, anything wrong?"

"Just the wind."

"You look cold."

"This silly dress." Then, feeling Tony's gaze on it, she remembered. More than silly. Ill-advised. Nearly ruinous.

"Janey, I thought you . . . you and Alan . . ."

"Don't even say it."

"But when Sheila told me. When I saw the dress—"

The door imperceptibly opened. Seeing his face, she could feel with him the impact of that moment when he had stood in his own living room and heard a teen-ager tell him about his wife's betrayal. About what he must have thought was a wife's betrayal. Then in her mind the scene shifted; it was Alan's chagrin she appropriated. Did Alan realize as soon as the designated train came in? Or, a man not used to being stood up, did he wait around another uncomfortable half hour until the next tired line straggled up the stairs? Alan knew so many angles, had so many ways of getting things done—he would have found a way of avoiding for someone else the useless wait in a dusty station.

"Tony, don't mention any of it again."

But when he moved toward the light, she saw his face. "I almost did something too. Something foolish. Yesterday morning I made a phone call. I have an appointment for Monday with—"

"Break the appointment. Whatever it is, break it." This time she was the one to curtail speech. When she kissed him, those past mistakes grew dimmer—for long periods it might be possible to believe they had never existed.

"Tony, such luck. Suppose you hadn't walked by here, might have been hours and hours before—"

Suddenly he was standing straight. "Not luck—I almost forgot."

"Forgot what?"

"I promised Doreen—she's right down there."

Down there . . . she had no idea what he meant, but the mention of Doreen, the sense of her presence, brought reality back. They were not a couple for whom nothing mattered but the thrilling submission to their own emotions; they were two people trying to wind up some unfinished business on a public embankment beyond which the clamor of a carnival had precedence. "Best seats on number nine bleachers. Choice seats still left on number nine," the loudspeaker blared, and she realized its hortatory words must have been issuing out the whole time. Its words, the revolving lights, the tinned music, the parents calling to their children. And Doreen—had she been here too, within a few feet of them? Was she never going to leave them alone?

"Down where?"

"That boat to the left. See it?"

Out of what had been an undifferentiated darkness, the vertical lines of masts took shape, shook like cautionary fingers before her gaze. "This one right here?"

"No, the cabin cruiser, with the blue stripes. Tied up at the end."

She couldn't make out the stripes, and of course he couldn't either, but when the wind stirred, a new set of reflections waved along the purple water. "What's she doing there?"

"Waiting for me to give her the money for the boat. Seven hundred and sixty dollars." He sighed. "She expected eight hundred, that's what was arranged, but the fellow took off forty because the seats were broken."

The anxious note in his voice showed that Doreen's presence had impinged on him too. Already, in his mind, he was phrasing the comforting words: Forty dollars less, Doreen, but he insisted, absolutely nothing I could do about it.

She couldn't tear her gaze from that amorphous shape at the end of the dock—it grew, in fact, less amorphous as she stared. "Very snappy boat. She know the people?"

"Not exactly. She saw them getting off; she knew they wouldn't be coming back tonight."

It was like Doreen: any stranger's boat lightly commissioned into involuntary service. "Tony, maybe she's watching us right now."

"She said she was exhausted, she'd go down to the cabin

and rest till I came back—maybe sleep." But he stood stiffly, not touching her—even the idea of Doreen's surveillance was enough to ruin their embrace. Suddenly, Doreen was all over —she was curled up in her yellow dress in the tidy elegance of some bunk, but she was also disclaiming in her shrill voice about the view, she was directing her wide-eyed gaze across the water, she was clutching a man's arm as she took mincing little steps across the planks.

"Let her sleep," Jane said sharply.

"I can't. She made me promise." He had moved further into the shadows—she peered at his indistinct face. "Jane, she felt terribly strong about it."

"Does she think you'll run off with her seven hundred and sixty dollars?"

"Don't ask me why. She just said it was important. The instant I got back—ten, ten-thirty—I should go in immediately and wake her up."

She was conscious again of the enveloping noise. The loud-speaker had stopped, but on the other side of the beach the promised firecrackers were under way—there were gentle popping sounds, then, poised with momentary brilliance against the blackness, sprays of pink-and-silver stars. "Suppose you don't wake her up?"

"You should have heard her. It was practically an obsession. I shouldn't waste a minute. It would be awful if I were late. I should come right down."

There it was again—Doreen's image with the head tilted to one side, the eyes importunate, the mouth drooping as she exacted the mollifying promise. "Can she get hurt, lying there?"

"Night like this, nothing can happen to the boat," he conceded.

"Will she be sick? Hungry? Thirsty?"

He had that look of one trying to be fair: even to a woman who had killed her husband, Tony would find it necessary to be fair. "She can drink whatever is in that thermos."

What was there about that thermos, so it kept on obtruding? Lorie's parents had tensed up, in some curious way, when they mentioned it, and here it was in the conversation once more. It was typical: even doing some simple act like borrowing a thermos from her neighbors and filling it with lemonade, or maybe lemonade and pineapple juice mixed, Doreen could manage to get herself attention.

"That is, she can drink it now, but she nearly didn't have it," Tony went on.

"How come?"

"She tried to give it to me. Take it, she kept saying—Go on, take it."

"Why didn't you?"

"I almost did. In fact, I had it. It and the bill of sale for the boat, and the rope from the anchor, and my sunglasses— all in my hand at the same time. And it was hot as hell and I knew after five minutes on that Sound I'd be dying to drink something. Anything. Even whatever kind of idiocy Doreen had concocted."

He paused a second, while another cluster of transitory stars broke against the sky, another image of Doreen broke against their unwilling minds. "I don't know . . . something about the sight of her standing there and smiling. That little smile, after what she'd done. I said I'd sell her boat, but I was goddamned if I would take her picnic food. Just as the boat pulled out I leaned over and set the thermos on the dock."

He sighed, as if that trivial act of defiance had been a satisfying token of his feeling, had, indeed, in some obscure way, made up for all the indignities that had gone before.

"Maybe the thermos is still there." She squinted at the dark outlines of the dock.

"No. She picked it up and reminded me about being on time. That's how I saw her last—the yellow thermos clutched against her yellow dress."

Doreen, leave us alone. Get out of our minds. Let us go home and make love without your interference. "Tony, if you wake her now, d'you really think that'll finish it?"

He stood silent against a tree.

"Not just a matter of waking her. She'll make complications. Cook up something. You know that."

"We could just—"

"With Doreen you can never just. There's always some unexpected trouble, something only she could think of. Besides" —she kept her eyes on his face—"we'll have to decide what to do about her. Whether to tell people. How to act."

She had been arguing for an evening's inviolability, but the import of what she had said was suddenly borne in on her. Not just a matter of handling whatever temperamental outburst Doreen put over tonight, but deciding how she should be handled for every day and night hereafter. Doreen had killed a man; deliberately, cunningly, she had put poison where her husband would be likely to drink it. No use prosecuting her, Mrs. Merimee had said: it wouldn't get Martin back and it wouldn't provide any personal vindication, and that was the end of it. But it wasn't the end. It couldn't be; the scene tonight with Lorie's parents had proved it. Doreen had not been present but she didn't have to be. Her talents for entwining herself around some strong man, arousing his sense of protectiveness, infuriating some other woman who found herself standing by useless—these familiar ingredients had all played themselves out in her cluttered living room.

Conceivably, that particular damage was finished. The man with the youthful face under the bald head was back with his own family. He was telling Pris not to cry—she was somehow sure of it—and diapering the baby, and pulling Robert off Henry's back; his wife, looking on, knew everything would be all right. But the next victim might not get off so easily. Next time it might be someone like Martin, who was susceptible enough to over-respond when a girl came up a mountain in sandals after him, sensitive enough to feel guilt when she put on her phony act. Doreen would go on and on, performing her little mischief at the point of men's greatest vulnerability —it would be up to them, Jane and Tony, to stop her. But should they stop her by telling people what they knew? Was it fair to the others who were involved? Doreen's potential menace against a young boy's mental health, the morality of punishment against the perils of exposure . . . there would be no easy decision, maybe not even a right one.

There would be no easy decision, but whatever it was, they could face it tomorrow. They could face Doreen then too. Even if she tried to insinuate herself back into their lives, they could handle it. The two of them together would listen to her explanations, weigh her protests, maybe even murmur in reluctant sympathy. Don't cry, Doreen, they would say.

But that was for tomorrow—tonight was something else. "Darling Tony, don't you see?—going down to that cabin will just start the complications again. Be another night Doreen will have ruined for us. Wrecked."

"I guess, if she's not here by now, she fell asleep."

She nodded. See you tomorrow, Doreen. We'll be up to meeting you then. Facing your problems. Figuring out what to do about you.

He took a last look at the swaying masts. "No reason she shouldn't sleep there till morning."

"Past morning. Till noon. Till we can make up for lost time."

His arm tightened around her. "Janey, love, let's get home fast." A final firecracker illumined the line of boats as they walked from the dock.

8